THE TEDDIES SAGA

· They Threw Us Away ·

THE TEDDIES SAGA

THEY THREW US AWAY

DANIEL KRAUS

illustrations by Rovina Cai

HENRY HOLT & COMPANY

NEW YORK

Henry Holt and Company, *Publishers since 1866*
Henry Holt® is a registered trademark of Macmillan Publishing Group, LLC

120 Broadway, New York, NY 10271 · mackids.com

Library of Congress Cataloging-in-Publication Data is available.

ISBN 978-1-250-22440-8

Our books may be purchased in bulk for promotional, educational, or
business use. Please contact your local bookseller or the Macmillan Corporate
and Premium Sales Department at (800) 221-7945 ext. 5442 or by email at
MacmillanSpecialMarkets@macmillan.com.

First edition, 2020 / Designed by Katie Klimowicz
Printed in the United States of America by LSC Communications,
Harrisonburg, Virginia
1   3   5   7   9   10   8   6   4   2

This book is for my sister Jenny.

I see stuffing in a big metal chest.
I see stuffing inside a twisted plastic nest.
I see stuffing piled along a cold gray floor.
I see stuffing in a crowded brown drawer.

THE HAZE

Buddy woke up.

Nothing was right, or as hoped, or as promised. He knew that instantly. The silky, humming, fluttering over-head lights of the Store had been replaced by unbroken yellow light. It was hot against his plush. It was dizzyingly bright. He covered his glass marble eyes with a paw.

Wait, that wasn't right either. He was able to move his paw to his eyes?

So far, Buddy had spent all his life inside a box. He knew its every inch. It had been narrow and rigid, with white plastic cords cuffing his paws to the cardboard. He'd been able to waggle his paws and feet, and turn his head a little, but that's it.

Now he was free.

It was a nice word, even fun to say: *freeeee*. All the teddies in the Store had wished to be free. All night, they'd whispered about being let out of their boxes. They deserved it! They were a very special kind of teddy. None of the other stuffed toys moved or talked. Even now, shielding his eyes from the sizzling gold light, Buddy felt good about being special.

Naturally, all the teddies at the Store had gone still and silent whenever a person entered their aisle. A grown-up shopper, a child, the people who mopped the floors at night—it didn't matter. Seeing a teddy move or talk might scare a person. That might make a teddy less likely to be chosen. And being chosen was all the teddies wanted.

Buddy wished teddies knew how to cry so he could release his longing to be back at the Store. The Store had been a vast castle stocked with rainbows of toys. Posable dolls with brushable hair. Sneering warriors throttling swords. Metal cars that—don't tell anyone!—were secretly robots.

Each day at the Store had been like fifty birthday parties at once. Children paraded down aisles. Buddy remembered his box had a circle cut through the front so children could pet his fur. *Pick me,* he used to pray. *Pick me because I pick you.*

Children had begged. Parents had peered. The orange teddy on Buddy's right: into a cart. The golden teddy on Buddy's left: into a cart. Buddy's turn had been coming. To a teddy, this was the meaning of *free*: being selected off the shelf, taken home, and embraced by a child.

When a teddy got that child's first loving hug, the teddy entered Forever Sleep.

Buddy yearned for it more than ever. Life was too rough for soft little teddies. What Buddy recalled of his birthplace was scary: a large, clattering room jostling with people handling more teddies

2

than Buddy could believe. After that had come a dark, rollicking truck bed loaded with teddy boxes. That was even scarier.

Forever Sleep would make all scares float away. Teddy rumor had it that Forever Sleep felt like a child's hug that never ended.

Nothing of the sort had happened yet. Buddy didn't remember a shopping cart, a child, a hug, any of it. He realized he was nervous to move his paw off his eyes. Wherever he was, it sure wasn't the Store. It sure wasn't a child's room. Something else had happened.

Buddy's plush was getting hotter.

There were no children here.

He peeked down at his body. It was strange to see himself outside his dark box. But all his parts were where they should be. His pudgy teddy limbs. His round tummy. His blue teddy fur. A tag was sewed to the seam at his side. *MY NAME IS BUDDY*, it read. Seeing his name printed like that made Buddy feel stronger.

He was still gazing at his belly when he detected a swishing sensation along his back. It felt like children petting him through his box's petting hole. Could it be that a child—*his* child, whom he'd somehow forgotten—was right behind him, playing a silly prank?

The swishing changed direction, messing the plush of his belly.

It was wind. Buddy had never felt wind before.

He was outdoors. That explained the hot yellow light. He'd seen the sun only once while being transferred from the shipping truck to the Store. It had been startling and beautiful—but now it frightened him. If only his box was near so he could scurry into its familiar darkness.

Yes, that was it! Maybe the box *was* near. If he waited inside it, surely someone would carry him back to the Store. Buddy had never liked the plastic cords strapping him inside his box, but now he missed them.

Being safe, he decided, was more important than being free.

The first step, though, was to look around. Buddy ordered his frightened, fluffy brain to do it. He let his blue paw slip off his glass eyes, stared through the sun, and saw the world.

2

Mountains reached up on all sides. Buddy had learned about mountains from people chatting at the Store. "Look at that mountain of boxes," they said. "I have mountains of work to do," they said. Mountains were big hills—but Buddy never imagined them *this* big. Already small, he felt even smaller.

The mountains were made of trash, an even bigger surprise. Trash was another thing Buddy knew about from the Store. At night, people swept and mopped the floors and tossed candy wrappers, Popsicle sticks, and more into a big, smelly barrel.

Buddy shuddered at the thought of so much trash in one place. He searched, hoping for a cheerier detail, but garbage coated every speck of land. He couldn't see any trees or rooftops. Just trash, near to far, low to high.

Beyond the rolling hills of waste, farther than the farthest peaks of junk, steam rose from hot garbage, turning the rest of the world into a greasy smudge.

Buddy instantly named this far-off smear the Haze.

The trashlands were too much for one teddy to absorb at once. Buddy focused on a garbage mound directly in front of him. It included plenty of boxes, though none were his. A few of the boxes had barfed out empty drink cans. Buddy sniffed the air with his plastic nose. Some of the cans smelled sugary; it made him think of children. Other cans smelled bready; it made him think of grown-ups.

Other uninvited odors—slick, stinging, slimy gobs of them—attacked his nose. Fruity smells, meaty smells, salty smells, chemical smells. New sounds were everywhere too. Birds chirping, insects whirring, the whooshing of distant trees. It made Buddy queasy. But if he was going to find his box, he needed to get moving.

Inside his box, he'd wiggled a lot. All teddies did. But he'd never walked. Carefully, Buddy pushed himself to his feet. He swayed a little but didn't fall. There, that wasn't so bad, was it? He cranked his paws around. Why, it was invigorating! Buddy tried hugging himself. He gasped. Hugging himself felt wonderful! No wonder children wanted to hug teddies.

He took his first step slowly along the foot of the hill. Quickly he understood why teddies were better off being carried. His head was too big and made him teeter. His legs were too soft to kick

6

aside a paper plate. His nubby tail wasn't big enough to help with balance. His stuffing pinched where his legs swung, and he wondered if the seams might rip.

Don't you fall apart, he ordered himself.

Buddy's confidence grew, bit by bit. He decided to try speaking, not in the teddy whispers of the Store, but loudly. He concentrated on what he was going to say. Once, he'd seen a pretty orange butterfly flutter into the Store. Now it felt like the butterfly had been sewn inside his chest.

"Is . . . anyone there? I think . . . I'm lost."

Buddy's voice was mild, yet he shivered in guilt. Walking and talking right out in the open—it just didn't seem right. Buddy doubled his determination to find his box. Once inside, there would be more no more misbehavior. He trained his eyes on his little blue legs so he wouldn't trip over the trashland's lumps, snarls, and mires.

The Store had been colorful but tidy. Trashland colors were abstract and spilled in every direction. Buddy's clean feet passed across all sorts of revolting rubbish. Soiled, wadded napkins. Plastic bags inhaling and exhaling with the breeze. Fast-food wrappers wounded with ketchup. Cotton swabs yellowed with earwax. Baggies of dog poop. Apple cores, banana peels, bread crusts. And water bottles by the billions.

Buddy felt the closing jaws of fright. How badly he needed that Forever Sleep hug!

His blue feet, designed for a child's bed or lap, began to soak a grubby brown. What would the Store think about grubby-brown teddy feet blotching their white shelves? Buddy's future child might get sent to their room if Buddy got too dirty. For Buddy, that was the final straw. Teddies simply were not built for adventure. There was no use trying. He should stop.

The half circles of his teddy ears perked up at an interesting crinkling sound. Well, traveling a few more inches couldn't hurt. He padded past a sun-blistered carton of laundry detergent.

Near the foot of a garbage hill was his box.

Buddy gasped and hurried as fast as his stubby legs could carry him. He jogged around a fly-covered pickle jar and clambered over the flab of an old bicycle tire. As he got closer, he realized one bad thing and one good.

Bad: It wasn't his box after all.

Good: It looked exactly like his box, and scattered upward along the hill were three more boxes just like it.

Trapped inside each of the four boxes was a teddy.

3

Without fingers, Buddy's paws were no good at ripping open factory-glued cardboard, and his legs were too fluffy to kick through the plastic window. He tried anyway. From inside, a teddy with yellow fur strained against her cuffs, her muzzle mashing flat against the window.

"Please hold on," Buddy said. "I'm trying my best."

The yellow teddy quit struggling. Her black nose popped back out of her face.

"Is something wrong?" Buddy asked.

"You're not whispering. You're walking. Those aren't things I'm used to."

"Me neither," Buddy said. He poked his paw through the petting hole. "Can you wiggle your paw through this?"

The yellow teddy snapped to attention. Buddy learned at the Store teddies came in all shades of colors, but otherwise were the same. And yet . . . wasn't this teddy different from him, just a bit? There was something bold about this yellow teddy. Maybe it was the slant of her forehead stitching. Maybe it was her eyes, embedded a little deeper in her face.

The yellow teddy crimped sideways before, quite suddenly, half her body collapsed into itself as she contorted toward the hole. Buddy winced. What if her body never recovered from all that twisting? The Store wouldn't like that.

The yellow teddy didn't hesitate. She wiggled, squashed, and shoved until a squat yellow paw sprang through the hole.

Buddy touched her paw.

"I'm Buddy," he said. "Pleased to meet you."

"Yes, I see your tag. Buddy is a very nice name for a teddy. Now, can we focus on getting me out of here?"

Buddy read her name off her tag: Sunny. It fit her color, if not her disposition. Sunny was bossy, though her bossiness got things done. It was Sunny, for instance, who used her paw to point out an empty can of peaches. The can's lid looked sharp, and Buddy didn't want to touch it. What if it slashed his fur? But Sunny insisted the lid was about to fall off, and sure enough, Buddy only had to touch it for it to snap free.

Wedging the can lid into the petting hole wasn't easy, and it smeared Buddy's paws with peach crud. But with Sunny's help, he sawed open several inches of cardboard. That was all Sunny needed to squeeze half her body outside, widening the slice like a moaning mouth. Next, Buddy used the peaches-can lid to sever the plastic cuffs.

Just like that, Sunny was freed into the world, first falling, second tumbling, and third standing on legs she'd never used.

"Thank you," Buddy sighed.

"Why are you thanking me?" Sunny asked. "Without you, I might have been trapped in there forever."

Buddy shrugged. "Because I was alone and scared."

Now that Sunny felt confident on her feet, she stood as straight as the toy soldiers Buddy had seen in the Store.

"I'll never forget this, blue teddy," the yellow teddy declared.

"Buddy," he reminded.

"You saved my teddy life. I vow to pay you back."

"You don't need to do—"

"It's a Teddy's Duty." Sunny tilted her head and grinned. Clearly she liked the sound of that phrase! She stood even straighter, standing on the front tips of her round feet. Her tail wagged to keep her steady. "That's right, a Teddy's Duty! I will not nap until all teddies in this disgusting place are safe in children's arms!"

Buddy was impressed.

"That sounds quite noble," he said. "But can I ask a question first?"

"I suppose you can."

Buddy gazed at Sunny hopefully. "Do you remember how we got here?"

Sunny's forehead pinched. "Let's see. I remember where we were born—all those workers, all those teddies, all those boxes. I also remember the truck. Of course I remember the Store." She shook her head. "Then everything goes black."

Buddy sighed. "Same for me."

"Now let me ask *you* something," Sunny said.

"I'd be delighted to answer," Buddy said.

"Why aren't you in a box like the rest of us?"

Sunny sounded suspicious. Buddy understood why. Her yellow limbs were still indented from her plastic cuffs, while he didn't have any marks on him at all. How long had Buddy been outside of his box? Who'd taken him out and why?

"I don't know," Buddy replied miserably. "Can I get a hug?"

"For Mother's sake, we don't have time," Sunny said. "Have you noticed the birds?"

"Birds?"

Sunny pointed a paw upward. Buddy leaned back so his eyes again warmed in the sun. Gradually he saw slender shapes melting through the Haze. Gulls, twenty or thirty of them flapping long wings in lazy circles. Some settled atop distant trash mountains, stabbing at garbage with curved beaks. Most flew haphazardly, black as ink, like the darkest parts of the world had taken flight.

"I see what you mean," Buddy said.

"A Teddy's Duty calls us!" Sunny reminded. "Quick, grab that lid."

4

The teddy inside the second box was the soothing mint green of an untouched tropical sea, or at least what Buddy's stuffed head *thought* a tropical sea might look like. On the way to him, a TV remote tripped up Sunny and an empty tissue box snared Buddy's leg, which gave the mint teddy time to prove that he wasn't soothing after all. Each time they fell, he wailed.

"Get up, you two! Be quick, be quick! There are *things* in the garbage! Living things, burrowing and snacking! I've seen them! If they get you, what will happen to *me*?"

Buddy thought it was a good thing he'd freed Sunny first, because the mint-green teddy was no help at all. If Buddy and Sunny had been dismayed to wake up in the stinking trashlands, this teddy was terrified.

"Come on, slowpokes!" he begged. "Don't just stand there!"

The green teddy's name was Horace. He shook so badly Sunny and Buddy had trouble handling the lid. Driven by her Teddy Duty, Sunny was about to make the surgical slice when the mint-green teddy banged on the plastic. The lid slipped, and its razor edge nicked the plush of Horace's left paw.

"I'm cut!" Horace cried. "Oh, Mother, this is the end! My tragic end!"

"I'm sorry," Sunny said sternly. "But if you don't quit moving, it might get worse."

Horace held himself tight, murmuring prayers. Buddy and Sunny finished the job and dragged him free. Buddy wanted to comfort Horace. But the green teddy wouldn't listen. He kept rocking in place. He also refused to follow them to the third box. So Buddy and Sunny nestled Horace inside a pizza box plastered with old cheese.

Buddy took another look at Horace's injured paw before glancing up at the gulls. Were there more gulls now? Were they closer, or was that fear talking? Buddy knew as much about gulls as he did tropical seas, but believed eyes as shiny as theirs would spot Horace's bright white stuffing from a mile away.

Sunny was halfway to the third box. Buddy pushed through belly-high garbage to catch up. He kept thinking of the "living things" Horace had seen under the garbage. When he joined Sunny at the box, the yellow teddy gave him a satisfied look, like she was pleased Buddy hadn't hidden inside the pizza box too.

It felt good to be relied upon. Buddy figured most teddies never got to feel it.

The day's fourth teddy didn't badger Buddy and Sunny to hurry. Instead, she watched serenely as they sawed through cardboard and plastic. Even when the lid sliced close to her face, she only giggled. *MY NAME IS SUGAR*, her tag read, and she was a lovely carnation pink.

"Are you trying to have snugs with me?" she asked hopefully.

"Snugs?" Buddy asked.

"You know," Sugar said. "Snugs? Snugging? Snug-a-wugs?"

"We're trying to get you out," Sunny said.

"I'll scoochy-poo to make room," Sugar said. "It's cozy-wozy."

"Didn't you hear what I just said?" Sunny asked.

"Wait till you see," Sugar giggled. "This box goes on forever. Like a lake. Like a dream."

"What is she gabbling on about?!" The closed pizza box dulled Horace's high-pitched whine from down the hill. "That kind of noise is going to get us all pecked apart by garbage gulls!"

Buddy and Sunny looked at each other. Horace wasn't helping, but he was right—something was off about this pink teddy. They got to work snipping her plastic cuffs. It helped that Sugar didn't flinch. She didn't seem brave exactly. It was more like she didn't understand the danger of sharp objects. Buddy worried Sugar wouldn't understand the dangers of the outside world either.

"That tickles," Sugar said when they cut the last cuff.

She didn't climb out, so Sunny and Buddy lifted her out by the paws. That's when they saw the damage. The top-right corner of Sugar's box was badly dented—someone had probably dropped it. That explained the sticker reading *DAMAGED MERCHANDISE*.

The box wasn't the only thing damaged. The top-right part of

Sugar's head was dented too. Her right ear was pushed all the way inside her head. The deformation drew her whole face tight and pulled her mouth into a quirky half smile.

"Oh, lookie!" Sugar laughed. "Look how the birdies go loop-de-loop-de-loop!"

The pink teddy might be acting silly, but Buddy and Sunny took her seriously. They checked the sky. Sure enough, fifty gulls had circled closer, honking and swooping, drawn by the teddies scurrying over the hill.

"Let's hurry," Sunny said.

"Let's," Buddy agreed.

"Let's be best friends," Sugar added—a nice thought, at least.

Buddy and Sugar rushed to the final box perched atop the hill. Sugar skipped after them, tra-la-la-ing. Horace shouted from inside his pizza-box bunker.

"Where are you all going?! Are you abandoning me?!"

The teddy inside the final box was gray. It made Buddy a little sad. Gray wasn't an exciting color. Most children probably wouldn't choose a gray teddy. Buddy felt bad thinking it, but the truth was, this teddy didn't seem exciting at all. While they worked to free him, he watched with none of Sunny's nerve, Horace's hysteria, or Sugar's misguided glee.

He politely introduced himself as Reginald, though when he spoke, Buddy didn't think he sounded like a boy teddy or a girl teddy. His voice was deeper than the others, which made Buddy wonder if he'd come to life before the rest and was a little older.

Even Reginald's box seemed older, white-veined with wrinkles, striped with bird poop, and stippled with coffee grounds.

Sunny slashed the box in half, and Buddy pulled Reginald out.

"Thanks," Reginald said. "I think."

Buddy didn't think Reginald was being sarcastic. He was being honest. Buddy decided to change his opinion. Gray might not be the flashiest of colors, but it was comforting. And wasn't comfort what a child wanted most from a teddy?

"See if you can contain all that excitement," Sunny told Reginald. "We need to run, right now, or we're going to be garbage too."

Buddy and Reginald followed Sunny's upward gaze, while five feet down the hill, Sugar lost control of her spinning and collapsed onto a corn-chip bag.

The fifty gulls had turned into one hundred, so many they blotted out the clouds. They squawked and nipped at one another's plumage. They were so close, Buddy could make out ghastly details. Wings curling like cutlasses. Black beaks and talons extending like needles. Merciless eyes sparkling like stolen gems. The gulls began to honk and blurt and, in a single black wave, dove at the defenseless teddies.

5

Teddies couldn't fight. It was a truth Buddy felt deep in his downy stuffing. Teddies were not in control of their fates at all. Anyone could pick them up or drop them, and if that included garbage gulls, there was nothing a teddy could do about it. Buddy gawked at the first bird coming at them with hurtling speed and hoped his teddy frailty would inspire birdie mercy.

In the seconds it took for the gull to reach him, Buddy saw its pinched beak, brute forehead, and pitiless eyes, and understood the beast had no mercy. The gull's alabaster wings spread like sudden night. Buddy could see dirt on the gull's outstretched feet and the broken shafts of individual feathers. The bird's knobby orange beak aimed at Buddy's chest.

A large, rectangular object slid between Buddy and the gull. The gull screeched. The object shuddered with the gull's impact and bopped Buddy in the face.

He fell back onto wet newspaper, bewildered by the disgruntled caw as the gull rebounded into the air. Buddy recognized the rectangular object as Reginald's box. Sunny had pushed it in front of them like a shield and was holding it in place with her paws.

"Teddy Duty," she murmured, struggling to keep it in place.

Reginald shoved his shoulders against it to help.

"We're not going make it," he observed.

The gulls screamed and circled, selecting new angles of attack.

"If you have a better idea," Sunny said, "I'd love to hear it."

Buddy didn't want a better idea. He didn't want any more ideas at all. Freeing these teddies had been the first idea he'd ever had, and it had led to this terror. The best idea now was to lie still and accept his fate like a teddy should. Buddy rolled to his side so he wouldn't be looking when the gulls came to carry them off to the Haze.

That's how he happened to notice the pink figure twirling halfway down the hill. The trashlands included every color imaginable, but a pink this pretty stood out. Buddy lifted his head to get a better look.

It was Sugar, skipping around a steering wheel like it was a merry-go-round. She didn't appear to notice how the sky had darkened with gulls, nor how the gulls' screeches had overtaken the trashland's buggy hum.

Buddy could accept being yanked into the sky.

He found he couldn't accept the same thing happening to Sugar.

"I have an idea." He blurted it before he'd even figured it out.

Multiple gulls flapped and pecked against the box braced up by Sunny and Reginald. Other birds were amassing in the air on the teddies' unprotected side, swooping in ovals, preparing strikes.

"Take your time," Sunny grunted.

"The box is split open where we cut it," Buddy explained. "Let's get in a line, the three of us, and push our heads inside it. The box will protect us while we run."

"Yes!" Sunny cried. "Did you ever see a toy turtle at the Store? Like that—like we're the feet of a turtle!"

Buddy pulled apart the cardboard and stuck his blue head into the box. It was Reginald's box, but it felt just like the one he used to have. The stuffy heat, the scent of brand-new plush, the way the clear plastic window smeared the world—its own little Haze.

Sunny's head popped into the box.

"They're getting close," she said. "Reginald! Get in here!"

In sprang Reginald's head.

"We're not going to make it," he reminded.

"Yes, we know." Sunny nodded at Buddy. "All right, boss. Lead on."

Buddy hesitated. Was this courageous yellow teddy calling *him* boss? The idea was preposterous. Buddy thought back to when Sunny asked where Buddy's box was. Maybe Sunny hadn't been suspicious. Maybe she'd been amazed.

What if Buddy had gotten out of his box *by himself*?

Oh, Mother, the idea was beyond ridiculous, and Buddy didn't have time for it. A gull swept past with a piercing shriek.

All three teddies ducked; the box ducked with them. Boss or not, Buddy had to lead, and now.

He took one step down the side of the hill. Walking was still a new sport, and his toeless feet skidded over eggshells and got tangled in a blender cord. Since the teddy trio was connected by the box, when Buddy stumbled, Sunny and Reginald stumbled too. The box swayed and nearly collapsed. Gulls squawked. Buddy trembled.

"You can do this, boss," Sunny whispered into his ear. "I believe in you."

Buddy bet teddies got lots of adoration from children. But he doubted any teddy had heard *this* before—that he might actually *do* something on his own. He peeked at the world beyond the box and pinpointed Sugar's dancing shape.

"Left foot, right foot!" he shouted. "Got it? Here we go. Left. Right. Left. Right."

There was some tripping, but it didn't last. The teddies fell into step—left, right, left—and like a cardboard tank with stuffed-animal wheels, they drove down the slope, dodging milk cartons, stamping sandwich crusts, and navigating the wobbly surface of a computer keyboard. Their advance angered the gulls, which dove like fighter planes, clawing the back of the box and twisting their necks for the teddies beneath.

"Sugar!" Buddy cried.

The pink teddy quit spinning. She plopped down on a water-bloated underwear catalog and waved hello. Shadows arrowed in her direction—gulls had spotted her and were closing in for the kill.

"Faster!" Buddy cried. "Left, right, left, right, left, right!"

Buddy would never forget the next few seconds. The teddies' six legs moved in such perfect coordination that their speed was doubled—no, tripled. Sugar's pink body blackened with gull shadows. Without Buddy having to give the order, the three teddies leapt in unison.

6

The box landed with a loud slap and a noxious cloud of kitchen chemicals. The cardboard edges cracked down perfectly, sealing Sugar safely beneath the box. The gulls screamed in frustration. The four teddies huddled inside the box, a turtle withdrawn into its shell. Their marble eyes flashed like pennies.

Buddy felt Sugar's hug.

"It's *you*," she sighed. "I missed you."

What had stiffened inside Buddy softened. He hadn't noticed that he'd been longing to hear these words.

"I missed you too, Sugar."

Sugar's high voice got even higher. "Can we go play with the green teddy now?"

"Horace," Sunny agreed. "Where's that pizza box?"

"We're not going to make it," Reginald added. "Have I mentioned that?"

"Nothing's going to get easier if we wait," Buddy said, and he was struck by the truth of it. If he'd never moved from the spot where he'd woken up, birds might have shredded all of them by now. "On three, we stand, all right? One, two, three!"

Sugar stood just fine—this was great fun!—but she was DAMAGED MERCHANDISE, and no good at telling left from right. Only Sunny's batting paws kept her from the gull beaks knifing along the box sides. Buddy spotted the pizza box and Horace's eyes gleaming from within, but realized Reginald was right. They'd never make it with Sugar's straggling.

"Sugar," Sunny said urgently. "Would you like a snug?"

Buddy turned so quickly the box plastic scratched a line through his face plush. Hugs were wonderful, but now was not the time!

"You bet I would!" Sugar bounded into Sunny's paws. "Snug-a-lug-a-lug-a-lug!"

Sunny looked at Buddy over Sugar's shoulder. Buddy understood: Sunny intended to carry Sugar this final stretch. Buddy was astonished. For a teddy to attempt that kind of physical feat was foolish.

Yet something told Buddy that Sunny, bound by Teddy Duty, might pull it off. Buddy believed in Sunny just like Sunny believed in Buddy. He had a feeling this shared trust was another thing most teddies never got to feel.

With a few shouted orders, Buddy got the group marching again. Each time Sunny had trouble with Sugar's weight, they swerved. But Buddy always steered them back, back, back. Their snaking path enraged the gulls, which bombarded with beak and claw.

Two feet before the teddies reached Horace, a gull landed on the box, driving all four teddies into a rotten-celery mush.

A large chunk of the box above them was torn off. Gleaming through the jagged hole were the gold-and-black eyes of a gull. A crooked scar zagged down the center of the gull's head. It spat the cardboard and stabbed its beak through the hole, barely missing Sunny's head.

"Run!" Sunny yelled.

Buddy didn't wait. He hurled the teddy box aside and sprinted for the pizza box, which Horace propped open with a paw. Buddy glimpsed Reginald running and heard Sunny coping with Sugar. He didn't dare look up but could tell from fattening shadows that gulls were diving. Buddy felt the heat of their bodies and smelled rancid trash in their claws.

Buddy lunged into the pizza box and slid across greasy cardboard. Reginald, quicker than he looked, landed at the same time, and they both grabbed on to Horace. Instantly, Buddy gasped. Dozens of ants covered Horace, munching his mint-green fur. Buddy slapped them away, and Reginald joined in, but already Buddy saw the damage: countless pockmarks disrupting Horace's perfect plush.

When Buddy looked up, he saw the worst thing they'd seen yet. Sunny was running over fish bones and shaving razors, pushing Sugar ahead of her, while dozens of gulls, bright red from the falling sun, dropped around them like a filthy blanket.

The gull with the jagged scar was closest. It spread its wings to the size of four teddies and thrust its purple-webbed feet at Sunny's back. Just then, Sunny threw herself and Sugar at the pizza box. Without thinking about it, Buddy shoved up on the pizza box lid.

It flew open, striking the gull's wing. The bird yawped. Its wing fluttered in a burst of dirty feathers.

All five teddies were sprawled across the pizza box—the *open* pizza box. Three more gulls shot at them like spears. Buddy went numb with fear, which allowed him to feel disappointment. The five of them had done things other teddies wouldn't believe. Too bad their luck had run out.

Three beaks struck in rapid sequence. The first hit Sunny's ear, the second Sugar's belly, the third Buddy's leg. Buddy waited to be yanked into the sky or feel his stuffing reeled out. Neither happened. Instead, the gull that attacked him flapped back into the sky.

Jiggling from its beak was a rubbery string of cheese. Buddy checked his leg. It hadn't really been hit. He saw the mark on the pizza box where the cheese had been plucked.

He looked at Sugar. Her belly was fine too, and she pointed mirthfully at the sky. Buddy followed the gesture to see the second gull fly away with a shriveled piece of pepperoni. Only Sunny had taken damage, though the new notch in her ear was no worse than the one on Horace's paw.

Buddy realized teddies were no match for old pizza when it came to bird appetites. That didn't mean the rest of the gulls would have such good aim. Dozens of gulls watched their colleagues make off with tasty morsels, and they wanted their share.

"Everyone up!" Buddy cried. "We need to hide!"

"Where?" Sunny shouted.

"Can't we just close the lid?" Horace pleaded.

"There," Reginald said.

Buddy followed the gray teddy's calm gaze and saw a large white cube planted in the trash. It was covered in rust, but Buddy identified it from toy versions at the Store. It was an oven. Plastic rings from a soda six-pack were caught in the burners and most of the oven dials were missing. The oven door, however, was slightly ajar, just enough room, Buddy thought, for teddies to squeeze through.

"The oven!" Buddy shouted, but Reginald was already scrambling for it, with the other teddies in pursuit. Reginald was the first inside and Horace the second, and the two helped pull in Sugar while Sunny pushed from behind.

"Tee-hee!" Sugar giggled. "That tickles my tail!"

Sunny glanced back at the rolling thundercloud of garbage gulls sweeping across the trashlands. Buddy wondered if the yellow teddy's torn ear ruined her chance of being restocked at the Store. Strangely, Buddy didn't think the ripped ear looked bad at all. It gave Sunny a daredevil look.

Sunny indicated the oven. "You first, boss."

"How did we . . . ?" Buddy began.

"Make it?" Sunny grinned. "We worked together. It's part of a Teddy's Duty."

Buddy pictured the boxes on his old Store shelf. All had held teddies, but each teddy had been kept separate by cardboard and plastic cuffs. Sunny was right. Finally allowed friendship, it was astonishing what a few little teddies could accomplish.

7

With the oven door shut, it was dark. The space was big enough for five teddies to stand, if they didn't mind bumping into one another. Buddy could tell they *didn't* mind. When the oven door gonged with the strike of a gull's beak, they drew together, hugging so tightly Buddy thought they looked like a single patchwork teddy stitched of blue, yellow, green, pink, and gray parts.

"This is a super-wooper snug," Sugar sighed.

Through a hole rusted in the door, Buddy saw the wrathful eyes of the scarred gull. Its claws scrabbled against the metal with an appalling *ping-ping-ping*. For the first time, Sugar became unhappy. She pressed her paws to her ears and made a high-pitched screech. When the gull flew away, Sugar stopped screeching, sat down happily, and hummed off-tune.

"We shouldn't be in here," Horace said. "Whose idea was this?"

Buddy knew what the green teddy meant. The place didn't feel right. Cracks in the walls leaked enough of sunset's glow for Buddy to look around. Everything was metal. In one corner, a dead light bulb stared blankly. Ash coated all surfaces. The place smelled bad, like burnt meat.

"Not too pleasant, eh?" Reginald's voice made cinder flakes fall like black snow.

Buddy joined him in the back corner.

"No," Buddy said softly, "but it *was* a good idea. How did you think of it?"

Reginald shrugged. "I know about ovens."

"I think I do too. But not as much as you."

"I know *lots* of things." Reginald sounded mystified. "Even things about how we ended up here. It's all buried inside my head. I can only see the edges of it."

"Is there anything I can do to help?"

"You're kind to offer. But I think it has to happen with time."

Buddy put a paw on Reginald's shoulder. "I'm glad you're here, Reginald. We're lucky to have you."

Reginald's marble eyes shone from the dark. "We're lucky to have *you*. I don't think you understand yet how lucky."

Yellow plush appeared behind them.

"I don't mean to disturb the chitchat," Sunny said. "But what now? Those birds are still out there, along with who knows what else."

"Maybe Reginald can tell us," Buddy said. "He *knows* things."

"Knows things?" Sunny scoffed. "I'm not going to risk my life on some gray teddy's hunches."

Buddy stepped forward. "There's no reason to be rude."

"I have my own hunch, boss. If we keep being polite like teddies usually are, we're never going to get out of this oven. At least we had a fighting chance outside!"

"Teddies don't quarrel," Horace pouted. He dipped a paw spotted from ant bites into a puddle of oily rainwater and scrubbed at a pepperoni stain.

Buddy agreed with Horace. Arguing tasted bitter inside Buddy's muzzle and sounded ugly in Buddy's ears. He was surprised, then, when he heard himself argue back.

"All right, Sunny," he challenged. "What would *you* like to do?"

Sunny jabbed her paw at the oven door. "Horace's box from the Store isn't far. Did anyone else notice our boxes have words printed all over them?"

Buddy looked down at his tag, which had the only four words he knew: *MY NAME IS BUDDY*. He noticed the other teddies checking their tags.

"We'll drag Horace's box in here and read it," Sunny said proudly.

Buddy hadn't considered it, but it seemed true: Teddies could read.

"The Store wouldn't put our boxes on their shelves unless every single word on them was true," Sunny concluded. "No offense, Reginald, but I trust the Store more than you."

Reginald shrugged. "Doesn't matter. Like I said, we're not going to make it."

"I don't think anyone should go out there," Buddy said. "Not right now."

"I wasn't asking for permission," Sunny grunted. "I'll do it myself."

"No one said they wouldn't help," Buddy sighed.

"Teddies don't quarrel," Horace murmured. *"Teddies don't quarrel."*

Buddy gave Horace a worried look before approaching the rusty hole in the oven door. Careful not to scratch his eye, he peered out. Plenty of birds still circled, but with every arc, more drifted back toward the Haze. The sun had narrowed to a scarlet squint. Buddy hadn't anticipated this loss of light. There had been no sun in the Store.

"The sun goes in the garbage too," Sugar said mournfully. "But don't worry. The morning mice will come, and they'll spill the garbage all over."

Buddy regarded Sugar's dented head with worry.

"I trust that even less than Reginald's hunches," Sunny said.

Buddy thought that was mean. He turned toward Sunny. "I'll give you a reason to wait until dark. No, fifty reasons. Maybe a hundred. The gulls."

Sunny cocked her head at the birds' savage honking, thought about it, then took a seat in the ash.

"I suppose it *has* been an eventful day. I guess I can wait a little longer."

Night brought with it more things for teddies to fear. It was too dark to see through the oven's cracks, but they could hear new beasts crawling from the Haze. Some sounded huge: Their lumbering bodies crushed egg cartons and plastic bottles. Others sounded small: Their tiny, clawed feet clicked across peanut shells and broken glass. No matter the beast's size, it ate. Every teddy heard the snuffling, gobbling, and gulping.

Buddy and Sunny stood for a long time with their ears pressed to the door.

"I think . . . ," Sunny said, "it's all clear?"

Buddy noticed Sunny had quit bragging that she'd do the job alone. Buddy listened, half hoping for a new beast to delay the mission. Sunny was right, though—it sounded safe. With Reginald's help, they pried open the oven door, and Sunny squeezed through, followed by Buddy.

The trashlands were lit by a powder-blue moon. Buddy stared at where the tallest trash mountains had stood. They'd vanished, as if they'd slid off a cliff.

"Boss!" Sunny hissed. "Snap out of it!"

Buddy shook himself from his trance and found Sunny pushing Horace's box. Garbage was piling up in front of it, slowing the progress. He hurried over and cleared the path of candy wrappers, medicine bottles, and yogurt cups. Then he lifted the front as Sunny lifted the back.

Reginald was waiting. He lowered the door with the help of Horace and Sugar, and together the five of them tumbled Horace's teddy box into the oven.

Buddy was the last teddy inside, and he heard, right before

the door closed behind him, the rapid patter of something dash-ing through the garbage. His instinct was to shake and cry. But words kept echoing in his cottony head. Sunny calling him *boss*. Sunny telling him, *I believe in you*. It might hurt to keep this fright to himself, but saving the others from it felt like something a leader would do.

8
.

They were hushed and respectful. Except for Horace. It was his box, after all, and he embraced it so hard—snugged it, Sugar might say—that one of the corners dug into his ant-bitten head. The others gathered close and by moonlight began to study the writing. As Sunny said, it was everywhere.

"Those words," Sugar said, "are a million-billion chocolate sprinkles."

Buddy realized Sugar couldn't read like the rest of them could. Sunny shook her head in dismay, but Buddy felt defensive. Sugar's head damage wasn't her fault!

Not wanting the happy-go-lucky pink teddy to feel inferior, Buddy read aloud the big, colorful words right above the plastic window.

"'Furrington Teddies.'"

"My, oh, my, how lovely," Sugar enthused. "Is that what I am?"

Buddy locked eyes with Reginald. Furrington Teddies? Did that sound right? The gray teddy nodded faintly.

"I guess so, Sugar," Buddy replied. "I guess that's what all of us are."

The other teddies began to stand a little taller. Buddy felt his back straighten too. To be part of a larger group, especially one with so fancy a name, made a teddy proud.

Buddy reminded himself not to get distracted. He proceeded down the box front. Where Horace's left paw had been cuffed was the petting hole. Buddy read aloud the words curved around it: "'Feel my fur. It's so-so-soft!'"

Sugar rubbed her tummy. "It's the softie-woftiest!"

"Thank Mother for that," Sunny grunted. "If it hadn't been for those holes in the boxes, we'd still be trapped."

"*Trapped?*" Horace sputtered. "Look at my plush! Look what those awful ants did to it! Every one of us ought to crawl back inside our box! They're the only safe places—can't you see that?"

Buddy imagined Sunny, Sugar, and Reginald scampering into the dark to return to their cardboard cartons. Having no box, Buddy would be left all alone in the oven. It was a worrisome thought, but for now all Buddy could do was keep reading. To the left of the petting hole was a sentence in large letters. Buddy read it aloud: "'I have my own name!'"

"Hold on," Sunny said. "Are you telling me non-Furrington teddies *don't* have names?"

"They must not," Buddy said. "Why else would they write that on the box?"

"We're special," Sugar sighed.

Two little words, but they had power. No one made a sound,

but Buddy felt warm pride radiate from their fur. They were Furrington Teddies. With So-So-Soft fur and Their Own Names. They were special all right.

He might have indulged the satisfaction longer if not for the teacherly sound of Reginald tapping the box. The gray teddy was calling attention to two tiny letters floating off the end of the word *Furrington*. Buddy surveyed the box and noticed those same two letters appeared everywhere the word was used: *Furrington*™.

"What's ™ stand for?" Sunny asked.

"Obviously it's an abbreviation of *thaumaturgic*," Reginald said.

"What?" Buddy asked. "Huh?" Sunny questioned. "Say again?" Horace asked. "Ooo!" Sugar squeaked.

"*Thaumaturgic* means 'one who works miracles,'" Reginald said.

"How in the world do you know that?" Buddy asked.

Reginald shrugged. "What else could it stand for?"

Sunny clapped her soft paws. "Why, sure! That explains everything! Don't you see? We're brand-new teddies, fresh from our boxes. Why would anyone throw away brand-new teddies? Brand-new *Furrington* Teddies?"

The others waited for the answer.

"They wouldn't!" Sunny exploded. "Someone made a mistake! Someone accidentally separated us from the children we're supposed to meet! But Furrington Teddies are thaum—thana—thamaburg—"

"Thaumaturgic," Reginald said.

"And that's why we have the courage to do all this walking and talking," Sunny concluded. "To keep ourselves safe until children find us. Once they do—well, there won't be any more of this stinky, dirty life for us! No, ma'am! We'll fall right into Forever Sleep, quick as you please. Doesn't that sound wonderful?"

Horace, still hugging the box, gazed up at Sunny, his hopeful eyes as vulnerable as water. Sugar snugged herself, acting out the embrace she'd soon get from a child. Reginald looked skeptical. Buddy thought he should be too. But he couldn't! The idea was too tantalizing.

Maybe it was Sunny's Teddy Duty that kept her on track. She hunched down to look at the right-side panel. Buddy huddled close to follow along as the yellow teddy read the words aloud.

Furrington™ Teddies DO . . .
- Snuggle
- Cuddle
- Nap
- Sleep

Sunny looked doubtful. "Aren't *snuggle* and *cuddle* the same thing?"

"I'm not sure," Reginald said. "*Nap* and *sleep* are different. If *sleep* means 'Forever Sleep.'"

"Put them all together and you have snugs!" Sugar cheered.

"Horace," Sunny called. "What's it say on your side?"

Reading the left-side panel meant Horace had to stop embracing the box. Therefore, it took a while. Sunny tapped her foot impatiently, and Sugar did a pretty good pirouette. After the mint-green teddy pulled away enough to read aloud the panel, his voice was as quizzical as Sunny's.

Furrington™ Teddies DON'T . . .
- Talk
- Walk
- Get in Trouble
- Be Mean

"I think we've broken all four rules already," Horace gasped.

"Easy, Horace," Sunny ordered, but Buddy could hear her uneasiness. Sunny did not, however, lose her nerve. "Be strong, Furrington Teddies! Don't forget how far we've come. We just have to . . ." Sunny shrugged. "Talk and walk and all that, just a little while longer."

Older layers of cinder hissed and crunched as Sunny rotated the box to look at the top panel. All that was there was a square with the notation *18 mo+*, and an orange sticker in the corner reading:

CLEARANCE
WAS $49.99
NOW $24.99

Sunny rotated the box again to display the bottom panel. Buddy was repelled by what he saw. It was different from the rest of the box. No cheery colors, no bouncy lettering, no fun at all. The dull white panel teemed with hundreds of tiny letters and numbers, like the lines of marching ants they'd seen in the trashlands. It wasn't intended for child eyes. Buddy knew it wasn't for teddy eyes either.

Everyone pitched in to help Sunny stand the box on end, although Sugar got distracted trying to snatch the red hearts printed on the side panels. Once the box was upright, the teddies let it fall front-first. It landed with a *whomp*, and a thousand flecks of soot took flight. Buddy used both paws to wipe it from his eyes, and as a result, he heard the others gasp before he saw their shocked, ashy faces.

The back of the box was dominated by a gorgeous photo of a Furrington Teddy on a child's lap. The child was sitting against pillows in a bed, with arms linked across the teddy's chest. Buddy's legs felt weaker than they had during his first trashlands steps. Here was everything he wanted, deep down in his stuffing. The cuddling of child and teddy was so cozy, so clean, so perfect. That's where he belonged, not drudging through disgusting waste.

One detail thrilled Buddy above all others. The teddy pictured was blue. Not yellow, not gray, not mint green, not carnation pink. Blue, just like him. His delight was chased by concern the other teddies would be jealous. First, Buddy came to life without a box—and now this? It was best not to mention it.

At the top of the back was a quote.

"'I'll be there when you need me,'" Buddy read aloud.

Buddy felt a throb of recognition. He knew this phrase. It lived inside him, as if it had been whispered into his stuffing upon his creation.

"We *will* be there," Sunny whispered. "Won't we? When we're needed?"

Buddy nodded. "I think we will."

"For the children," Horace peeped.

"For one another," Buddy added.

"That's what a Furrington Teddy *does*," Sugar insisted, waving exasperated paws.

Buddy smiled. How lucky he was to have met this stellar group of teddies! He returned to the box. Alongside the child's face was a fluffy cloud shape printed with three sentences. Buddy read them aloud.

Congratulations on your Furrington™ Teddy.
No teddy is made with more care.
Each Furrington™ Teddy has a Real Silk Heart inside!

The oven resounded with gasps.

Buddy looked up to find Horace prodding his springy chest with his nubby paws. Seconds later, Sugar and Sunny did the same, poking their own plushy torsos. Reginald gave his body a dubious look, but even he couldn't resist giving it a nudge. Buddy considered the globe of his own belly and gave it a poke.

"Anyone feel it?" Sunny asked in a hush. "Anyone feel a heart?"

"Real Silk Heart," Horace clarified. "I think perhaps I feel something?"

"I'm not sure," Reginald said.

"I doooooooo," Sugar sang.

For a breathtaking second, Buddy believed he did! But when he tried to find his Real Silk Heart again, he couldn't.

"They must be in there," Sunny deduced. "It must be what makes us therma—thuba—thumpa—"

"Thaumaturgic," Reginald finished. "And maybe . . ."

Buddy gestured for him to continue. "Maybe what?"

"Maybe the point is we *can't* see or feel our hearts. We have to have faith they're inside us. If we can have faith in our Real Silk Hearts, we can have faith in ™ magic too. Maybe it's that faith that *makes* us magic, that *makes* us thaumaturges."

Buddy wished his mouth wasn't stitched shut. He wanted to grin as widely as every birthday child he'd seen bouncing through the aisles of the Store. Reginald, that gray cynic, was beginning to change his tune! The teddies murmured in approval, then began to cheer. It was so exhilarating, the walls of the oven seemed to lift away, transforming the charred metal ceiling into a starlit sky.

9

The thrill of the box's secrets exhausted the five little teddies. Sugar dropped to her tail, still searching her stuffing for her Real Silk Heart, and moments later, she was curled up on the dirty floor. Buddy saw Sunny stretching her paws, Reginald rubbing his eyes, and Horace gazing longingly through the window of his old box until, unable to resist, he wiggled inside.

Buddy had to admit the ant-eaten teddy looked happier in there.

The other four hunkered down in separate spots. But they were teddies, and before long they'd rolled back together, Sugar's leg touching Sunny's paw, Sunny's head touching Buddy's back, and Buddy's leg touching Reginald's tail. They all touched Horace's box, inside which Horace snored.

Buddy was glad they were touching. They were doing what the Furrington slogan promised: *I'll be there when you need me.*

Time passed, none of it quiet. Unknown Haze beasts stirred and snorted. Claws, small but wicked, ticked across the stove burners. In the distance—but not *so* distant—something howled, a prolonged, ghostly wail. Buddy shuddered and recalled the first words he'd spoken after coming to life: *Is anyone there?*

"Boss," Sunny whispered. "You awake?"

"Yes." Buddy was relieved to hear her voice. "Are you?"

"I'm whispering to you, aren't I?"

"Those noises. They're scary."

"They're . . ." Sunny wasn't the sort to admit fear. ". . . not nice."

"Maybe we should talk. You know, to distract ourselves."

Buddy thought he saw Sunny frown.

"What do teddies have to talk about?" she asked. "We're *teddies*."

"Tell me about yourself," Buddy said. "Please?"

"Buddy, you're talking nonsense. You know everything I know. My name is Sunny. I'm yellow. I came in a box. That's it. We're all the same, you numbskull."

"That's what I used to think," Buddy said. "But it can't be true."

"Why can't it?"

"For starters, I'd never call you 'numbskull.'"

"Oh, Mother. I'm sorry I started this conversation."

"But I'd *also* never have thought of using the lid to free the others. Or block the garbage gulls with Reginald's box."

"Well, thank you," Sunny grumbled. "I suppose I never would have thought of using Reginald's box as a turtle shell either."

"We're different," Buddy declared. "And I bet we keep getting different-er."

"Humph," Sunny grunted. "I hope that's a good thing."

44

Soot rasped as Buddy rolled over. "How could it not be?"

Before Buddy could ask what Sunny meant, another howl split the trashlands.

"Beasties have their own hearts," Sugar squeaked from the dark. "But they want ours too."

Another distressing idea. Just what Buddy needed. He and his friends were *still* a unified group, he reminded himself. They were *still* thaumaturgic Furrington Teddies with Real Silk Hearts and So-So-Soft fur. But it was also true they were lost in a harsh world. What if it took days for children to find them? Or weeks? How long could teddies last on their own?

"Reginald," Buddy whispered. "You up too?"

"It is impossible to nap," Reginald replied testily, "with all this whispering."

"I was wondering," Buddy said. "How come you know so much stuff?"

"Good question," Sunny added. "It doesn't seem fair."

"I think," Reginald said, "it has to do with this."

He patted the bottom of Horace's box. It was the panel Buddy disliked, the one crowded with minuscule numbers and letters. In the moonlight glow, Reginald indicated a bizarre symbol: a square holding a series of vertical black lines and a string of numbers.

"This is a code," Reginald explained. "The Store uses it to know which toys they have and how much the toys cost. I think my number came before all of yours. I think I was at the Store longer."

"If you were there so long, why didn't a child take you?" Sunny asked.

Sugar sighed. "No one wants a graysy-waysy teddy."

Buddy was mortified for Reginald. But the gray teddy didn't sound upset.

"Do any of you remember stories about the Mother?" he asked.

"The Mother . . . ," Sunny echoed. "I keep saying that: 'Oh, Mother.' I don't know why."

Reginald continued. "What about Proto and the Originals?"

"Proto?!" Horace sputtered from inside the box. "Is that a name?"

"The Originals . . . ," Buddy repeated. "Do you mean the original teddies?"

Reginald nodded.

The Mother, Proto, the Originals—these characters were buried deep inside Buddy's head stuffing. Had they lived before the Store? Before boxes? Even before Forever Sleep?

"I bet all of you remember the tales in time," Reginald said. "For now, I can tell you one. It's a story about where we came from."

"Eeeee!" Sugar squealed. "A story! A story with snugs!"

"Sugar," Buddy cautioned, "no one said it'll have snugs."

Sugar pouted and muttered "I bet it has snugs."

"Tell it already," Sunny urged.

"All right." Reginald's low voice was ideal for storytelling. "I'm going to tell you—I'm going to *remind* you—how it all began. It starts with the Mother."

10

ONCE UPON A dream and far away, the Mother was lonely. A teddy like you is probably surprised the Mother could get lonely. She was, after all, a Creator, and all Creators had gifts.

The Mother's gift was sewing, and she was proud of it. Nevertheless, loneliness lingered. One day, she cried so much that tears ruined her favorite dress. When she went to her sewing room to mend it, she noticed among her supplies a bolt of the Softest Fabric in the World.

Not everyone has the Softest Fabric in the World just sitting in their home. But it wasn't so surprising for the Mother.

She didn't have much money. She only had a few television channels. Her house was in disrepair, and she was too old for ladders and hammers. But when it came to sewing, she had everything she needed . . . and even a few things she didn't know she needed.

The Mother picked up the Softest Fabric in the World in her strong hands, stroked it, and the idea came to her all at once, like the best ideas usually do. She would sew herself a companion so she'd never feel lonely again.

There is no telling how she did it. It wouldn't make sense to teddies like us anyway. All we know is the Mother sewed all day and all night. Her sewing table shook so hard it rattled neighbors' dishes from shelves. Her needle and thread squeaked so loudly dogs down the block lost their minds. Her thimbles broke, and soon the white fabric was spotted with blood. She blotted and wiped, but some of it soaked in.

After a time, the Mother beheld her creation. It was a teddy. He had pure white fur, a big, round teddy head, a darling teddy frown, and intelligent teddy eyes. Naturally, he was also soft—softer than feathers, snow, petals, or secrets. She pet him and his fur crackled with static. She saw a little bolt of electricity.

The teddy looked up at her.

He did not hold still or stay quiet like we teddies of the future.

"Hello," he said.

"Hello," she said.

He looked around. "Did you make me?"

She replied, "Yes, I did."

He thought about that. "Would you like to have a tea party?"

She replied, "Yes, I would."

And so they had a tea party. And story time. And a pillow fight. And nap time. And collected rocks. And fed the goldfish. And napped again. And played dress-up. And went on an adventure. And watched birds. And made cookies. And napped again. And listened to music. And invented dances. And drew pictures. And made a

fort. And got ready for bed. And stayed up late. And watched TV. And made up jokes. And fell asleep in each other's arms.

When they woke up, they loved each other. She named him Proto. Their life together was grand. When rain drove down like nails, the Mother no longer wrapped herself in a blanket and felt sad. She and Proto watched the rain together and made up stories about people they saw under umbrellas. When the Mother watched movie scenes that upset her, they no longer burrowed into her head. She and Proto discussed the scenes, which made movies even better.

In short, the Mother was happy. It didn't matter she didn't have much money. She had a friend, and that was more important.

Proto was happy too. He was there when the Mother scrubbed dishes. He was there when the Mother paid bills. He was there when the Mother cleaned the toilet. All this may sound dull to you, but anything can be interesting if you're curious enough.

Proto was *very* curious.

One soggy morning, the Mother was in bed sniffling from a cold while Proto fetched her slippers, just like usual. He dropped them off and turned to fetch her favorite teacup. This time, though, he paused.

"You enjoy putting on your fuzzy-wuzzy slippers, don't you?" Proto asked.

"Why, Proto," the Mother replied. "You know I do."

"And you enjoy drinking from your favorite cup, don't you?"

"These are silly questions."

Proto shrugged casually. But he was a crafty teddy. In fact, he would become the craftiest teddy that ever was.

"I was just thinking," he said, "your enjoyment would be doubled if you got your fuzzy-wuzzy slippers and your favorite cup at the same time."

"That's not necessary, Proto. I don't mind waiting."

"If you got your fuzzy-wuzzy slippers and favorite teacup at the same time, then I could bring you your crocheting faster, and we could get to snuggling sooner."

"Life isn't about getting things done quickly," the Mother warned.

Proto nodded but didn't really listen. In truth, Proto wasn't a good listener.

"With just a few more teddies around here, we'd be able to have a million, billion, zillion more good times. We'd fetch your fuzzy-wuzzy slippers, and your favorite teacup, and rub both of your feet, and set up our card game, and read to you from books, and when you got sick—and let's face it, you're not getting any younger—we'd bring you tissues, and mentholated rub, and chicken soup, and aspirin, and—"

"Am I not enough for you anymore?" the Mother asked. Suddenly she looked sad, though it might have been her cold.

Proto rushed to her side and stroked her sweaty hair. "Balderdash," he insisted. "But I'm afraid it's the only solution."

The Mother sighed, then coughed, then sniffled. "All right."

Proto couldn't believe his furry ears. "Really? Oh, I'll—I mean you'll—*we'll* be so happy!"

He tossed himself into her arms, hugging her as hard as he could, no matter what icky stuff dripped from her poor red nose. The Mother hugged him back, but you can probably tell why she agreed to his idea. It wasn't to make herself happier. It was to make *Proto* happier.

The eight teddies she sewed were unrivaled in quality. You wouldn't expect anything less from the Mother. Being new, the eight teddies didn't have much personality yet, but the Mother admitted it was agreeable having helpers waddling around on adorable teddy legs. Proto was overjoyed and had a splendid time ordering the younger teddies around. They looked just like him, which was very flattering.

He came to think of them as "the Originals."

Pretty soon, the Originals weren't spending much time fetching fuzzy-wuzzy slippers or setting up card games. Sometimes they were even late for tea parties. When the Mother searched for them, grumpy without slippers and parched from lack of tea, she always found the same thing: Proto basking in the Originals' beauty and the Originals basking back.

The Mother began to worry. Her teddies were special—they walked and talked. Nine was a lot of teddies, and it was only a matter of time before one of them danced in front of a window or cavorted into the front yard. People would see and demand to know the Mother's secret. They might take the teddies away. They might even take away the Softest Fabric in the World.

She decided making the Originals had been a mistake. She couldn't give them away, as people wouldn't understand their walking and talking. So one night, with Proto and the Originals snuggled beside her, she settled upon her dreadful decision. The eight new teddies would have to be destroyed.

Now, you're a teddy. You know we're not the smartest folk in the world. But we can tell when someone's sad, or angry, or happy. Proto, the smartest teddy of all, sensed something awry with the Mother the following day. Instead of doing his chores, he tiptoed to the den to see what the Mother was up to.

Proto was horrified. The Mother was stabbing an iron poker into the fireplace. Beside her were a seam ripper and a pair of sewing shears. She was going to disembowel the Originals and burn their parts in the fire, until their plush turned to ash, their plastic noses melted, and their marble eyes popped like chestnuts.

Proto liked having the Originals around. Since he had the best personality, the other teddies adored him and paid him endless compliments. But how could he save them? Just as the Mother set down the poker, he had a risky idea.

He strolled into the den.

"Ah," he said. "I see you're planning to get rid of the other teddies."

The Mother looked at him in shock. Before she could deny it, Proto ran his paws over the seam ripper and shears.

"High quality," he praised. "These will work quite well."

"You're . . . not upset?" the Mother ventured.

"Upset?" Proto replied. "Balderdash! Why, I was going to suggest this myself. Those teddies have infested this place like mice. Shall we gather them up?"

The Mother might have been suspicious if the whole task hadn't gotten her so depressed. Proto whistled as he walked about, beckoning the Originals until he was trailing a line of eight portly waddlers. Proto instructed them to sit in a line on the hearth. It was winter and the crackling fire behind them made the teddies cozy-wozy.

"All right," Proto said. "Let's get started."

The Mother looked doubtfully at her seam ripper.

"One more thing," Proto said. "While you, ahem, take care of business, I'm going to get a head start digging eight friendly little graves for their remains. Surely they have been good enough teddies to deserve that?"

The Mother nodded sadly. Friendly little graves were the least she could do.

"Stupendous!" he said. "Now, to keep the graves straight, I'm going to have to mark them with names. Would you mind stitching names to their bellies so I can tell who is who?"

How could the Mother turn down such a harmless last request?

Proto watched her give the Originals a long look, scanning their bodies for differences no one else could notice. Proto was panicked enough to faint but made himself mosey from the den like he was jazzed to dig those holes. Several nervous seconds passed before he heard the Mother tick off the list of names.

"Geoffrey. Jasmine. Ulric. Anita. Edmund. Beatrix. Antwan. Sheila."

Naturally Proto didn't dig any friendly little graves. He crept back to the den to watch the Mother stitch name tags to the side of each teddy's stomach. For a Creator like her, it was easy work—so easy, in fact, she was caught off guard by the effect.

Once names were attached to the teddies, their differences, so trifling moments ago, became brazenly obvious. Geoffrey was taller than the rest. Anita's mouth curled upward a bit. Antwan's marble eyes were a handsome swirl of brown and green.

They were individuals.

Once you see a group as individuals, it becomes harder to hurt them.

The Originals swarmed over the Mother's lap to hug her, bursting with pride over their new names. Proto tiptoed from his hiding place. The Mother saw him and narrowed her eyes. Proto dipped his head in apology. But with so many soft teddies cuddling her, the Mother couldn't glare for long. She pet teddy heads and tickled teddy bellies—and shook her head at clever Proto.

He knew what the head shake meant.

It meant he'd won this round but shouldn't expect to win them all.

That was all right with Proto. Teddies, as you know, aren't so good at looking to the future. But they are *great* at celebrating right now. Proto bounced over to his friends Geoffrey, Jasmine, Ulric, Anita, Edmund, Beatrix, Antwan, and Sheila, and together with the Mother, they embraced and played and laughed until it was time for bed.

Buddy woke from his nap to clanging metal.

He'd been dreaming of Proto, that merry trickster who made himself a pest to the Mother in a dozen ways—but never so much she didn't still love him. Did this mean it was okay if teddies weren't perfect? Buddy hoped so. He wasn't a trouble-maker like Proto, but he envied the original teddy. The early days of the Originals must have been exciting, back when teddies moved and talked all the time, and Forever Sleep didn't exist.

Golden morning light revealed a harsh reality. Instead of a bedspread full of toys, Buddy saw the shark-tooth shapes of the oven's crust. Horace's box, so fantastical the night before, looked bent and battered, a reminder how rapidly the teddies had gone from clean and new to soiled and stinking.

Metal clanged some more. Buddy sat up and found Sunny by the oven door. She looked weird, and it took drowsy Buddy a min-ute to figure it out.

The yellow teddy had squeezed herself into a can missing both ends. Her head and legs remained big and poofy, which gave her a barbell shape. She also wore toilet paper rolls over her arms and legs. Topping off the bizarre garb was a thermos lid she wore as a helmet.

The thing making all the noise was a butter knife, which Sunny struggled to hold between her fingerless paws. It kept clanging the can.

"Why are you dressed like that?" Buddy whispered.

Sunny dropped the butter knife. It cymbaled off the oven floor. Reginald tossed in the ash. Inside his box, Horace groaned.

"It's armor," Sunny hissed.

Buddy couldn't help it. He laughed.

"Armor? You look like you woke up in a trash can."

Sunny frowned. "In case you didn't notice, we *live* in a giant trash can."

"True. But you don't have to dress up in it."

Sunny's frown quivered. She couldn't hold it back: She laughed too.

"All right, I look ridiculous. But give me some credit, huh? I went outside bright and early to gather this stuff. That's a Teddy's Duty. And I'm glad I did. Take a look."

Sunny jerked her head at the oven door. Buddy got up. Fear from the night before flooded back. But also a surprise strength. Here he was, walking and talking again, without a thought. He peeked through a crack at the sunlit trashlands.

Sugar stood a good distance away. As usual, she was oblivious to danger. She'd made a tiara from tinfoil, and it sat askew on her

dented head. In her paws she carried soda-can tabs like a bouquet. She skipped joyfully across a rotten signboard, somehow evading every rusty nail, and bent to sniff fast-food mustard packets like they were a bed of roses.

To Buddy's surprise, he wished he were out there doing the same. Sugar might be *DAMAGED MERCHANDISE*, but she was happy, just like a teddy should be.

"I'm going to bring her back," Sunny said. "And then? Then I'm going to climb that."

She jabbed the butter knife skyward. Buddy followed the gesture. Looming beyond the hill where he'd found the teddies in their boxes was the tallest of all trashlands mountains. It towered from behind a gauzy curtain of mist.

"That's impossible," Buddy said.

"The story Reginald told last night wasn't just for fun. We're supposed to learn from it. Proto didn't sit around and wait for the Mother to unsew the teddies, did he? No, sir. He did something about it. If I can make it to the top of that mountain, I'll be able to see everything. I'll figure out where we are. Better yet, I'll figure out where the nearest *children* are. Maybe I can even send them a signal."

"But the gulls . . . the Haze beasts . . ."

Sunny grinned and tapped the butter knife against her thermos lid. "That's why the armor. Anything tries to take a bite of me, they'll be sorry."

The yellow teddy kept surprising Buddy. Sunny knew the long

odds of their survival but refused to shrink in fear. She saluted with the knife and began opening the oven door.

Buddy heard the words burst out of him: "I'm going with you."

Sunny frowned at Buddy's armor-free body. "Now, look, boss—"

"I'd like to come too." Reginald was standing and brushing black ash from his gray fur. He noticed Sunny's irritation. "You said yourself I know things the rest of you don't. I might come in handy."

"Now, look, you numbskulls—" Sunny started.

"I'm not staying in this wretched place by my lonesome!" Horace popped his head from the box. His ant bites looked no better. "If the rest of you are running off, I am too!"

Sunny groused in a way that wasn't very teddy-like.

"Oh, fine," she said. "If Haze beasts attack, I'll try to make them come after me. But each of you is taking your own risk out there. Got it?"

With the armored Sunny in the lead, the teddies filed into the blazing sunlight and picked their way across the spongy trashlands. Noises kept them anxious. The gentlest breeze crinkled plastic and sent small things rolling down big piles. Birds sang, tweeted, and called, though not aggressively. The ones Buddy saw were more interested in selecting tasty litter than watching teddies.

First they corralled Sugar, who was so overjoyed to see them, she dropped her pop-top bouquet. (She kept the tinfoil tiara.) Next, the five teddies trekked past several hills and halted at the foot of the tallest trash mountain.

Buddy glanced at Sunny. Under her thermos-lid helmet, she looked plenty worried. The other teddies pressed close. Buddy felt them shaking. He noticed he was shaking too. It must be their Real Silk Hearts, he thought, pounding away.

"If we're going to attempt this cockamamie climb," Horace said, "let's get started."

Horace probably said it because standing there was dangerous. But it spurred Sunny into action. She squared her shoulders above the toilet-paper rolls, stuck out her can-covered chest, and took the first steps up the slope.

It was rough going. The heat applied to their fur like a thick coat of paint. Their marble eyes ached from watching for gulls.

That was only the start. A strand of holiday garland got knotted around Buddy's waist. Sugar fell between soda bottles that squeezed her like dough. A cardboard box collapsed beneath Sunny, and the others had to pool their strength to lift her out. Only Reginald avoided accidents. He traveled slowly, far behind the others, selecting the safest, cleanest steps.

The whole day passed. Or maybe only a half hour. Teddies, Buddy began to realize, were lousy at measuring time. He'd begun to think they'd never reach the top, when Sunny, who'd taken to using the butter knife as a walking stick, began waving it.

"The summit!" she cried. "It's right there!"

Buddy dragged his eyes past a broken high chair and a stained rug. Jutting from the peak of the mountain was a busted tennis racket. Energy surged through his stuffing, and he scrambled upward. They all did, ignoring the slimes soaking into their fur.

Sugar scaled the fastest, her tinfoil tiara twinkling. She reached the tennis racket before the rest.

"It's the world!" Sugar spun in circles. "It's the whole wooooorld!"

Sunny was the second to reach the peak. Buddy watched her halt Sugar's hazardous spinning before taking in the view. The butter knife slid from Sunny's grip. Her paw, now empty, reached for the tennis racket for support. Buddy drove his stubby legs harder and reached the peak along with Horace. Wind fluttered Buddy's fur as he took in the panoramic view.

There were no candy-colored houses where children might live.

There was no sparkling Store where teddies might be welcome.

There were only trashlands, as far as the eye could see.

Buddy had thought he understood trash. It came from garbage cans. If you had enough cans, you could create a pile, even a mountain.

But this was *a mountain range*. Trash spread for miles in every direction until it faded into the Haze. There were so many peaks of trash that, way down below, squiggly paths had been carved through them. The paths reminded Buddy of the threads that had started to spring from his stitching.

Don't you fall apart, he'd once told himself.

But everything was falling apart.

The summit was striped by ice cream bars that had melted into chocolate, vanilla, and strawberry streaks. This made it a yucky place to sit, but Sunny sat anyway. Buddy watched as she tossed her thermos-cap helmet, flapped her limbs free of the toilet-paper tubes, and wiggled herself from the metal can. After that, she didn't move.

Horace and Sugar sat down too.

Only Buddy didn't sit. He peered at the distant ground. In one direction, he made out a metal sign that read *GARDEN C*. In another direction, he found a sign reading *GARDEN D*. Trash peaks blocked additional views, though Buddy discovered one more sign at the foot of their mountain.

"'Garden E,'" he read. "Our area is called Garden E."

"Doesn't look like a garden to me," Sunny grumbled.

Ice cream bar wrappers crackled. Buddy whirled around, expecting ambush, but it was only Reginald reaching the peak at last. He showed no surprise at the gloomy view.

"Maybe this was a garden once," he said. "Maybe children used to play here. But it's a landfill now." He shrugged. "I told you we're not going to make it."

"Landfill?" Horace repeated. "What's a landfill?"

"It's a place where the earth is filled with garbage," Reginald replied. "It's loose like this at first, but then people squash it and bury it."

"They *bury* garbage?" Horace sputtered. "In the *ground*? Why?"

"If you bury it, up come garbage flowers," Sugar said. "I picked a whole bunch."

"I don't know why they bury it," Reginald admitted. "Maybe they think it makes it go away."

"Trashlands, garbage dump, landfill—what's the difference?"

63

Sunny asked quietly. "Garden E is our home now. Children will never find us here. We might as well accept our fates."

"No," Buddy said.

The other teddies looked at him.

Buddy was afraid. But he also felt stubborn. If Proto were here, he wouldn't give up without a fight. Buddy's fear began to melt like the sun had melted the ice cream bars. He and his friends had come too far to quit, and his job as boss was to make the others believe that—never mind the garbage gulls beginning to emerge from the Haze.

Buddy's Real Silk Heart swelled with ™ magic.

"Listen to me, Furrington Teddies." Echoing in the valley below, his voice was stronger than he expected. "If children aren't going to find *us* . . . then we'll find *them*."

12
•

The second the sun speared through the rust holes, Buddy and Sunny kicked open the oven door. It fell with a crash, scattering rust. The teddies had no armor, no weapons, no supplies, and no plans except one: Get out of the trashlands and don't stop moving until they found children.

Horace, Reginald, and Sugar lined up on either side. The red sun made heroes of them all.

"Whoopity-doo!" Sugar cheered. "So many fun ways to go!"

"But which one?" Buddy pondered.

"Whichever way you choose, I'll be right beside you, boss," Sunny said.

"We all will," Horace added. His trembling voice only made Buddy prouder.

"But if I may suggest a direction," Reginald said, pointing, "how about that way? Those dark shapes just might be treetops."

Buddy nodded. "No matter which way we go, this trash has to end sometime."

Holding paws, the five jumped toward trash slick with dew and honeyed with golden morning light. They landed with a crash so hard it shook the world.

It wasn't them, of course. Teddies are too lightweight. The crashes kept coming and coming, shaking Garden E hard enough to knock over Horace and Reginald. The teddies looked at one another in confusion.

"Uh-oh." Sugar gasped. "Did the Mr. Sun bop into Mrs. Moon?"

Every shred of garbage shuddered, from curtain rods to soiled diapers to shriveled tea bags. Something terrible came on dinosaur feet.

The tallest mountain in the trashlands, the one they'd climbed together, began to sway. Buddy couldn't believe the sight. An entire mountain moving? Impossible! Yet there it went, wobbling like a stack of dirty dishes. Rubbish began peeling off. Rodents bounded from hidey-holes and ran for their lives.

Bending metal, snapping plastic, splintering wood, and squishing slop all combined to make a single groan—and the mountain collapsed with a wet, deafening blast. All five teddies were jarred an inch from the ground. They landed on their faces, their tails.

Was this what the crashing sounds were? The destruction of the whole world? Buddy thought it was an unfair thing to make little teddies witness.

But all five Furrington Teddies *did* see it. Dirt, dust, soot, slime, and mold mushroomed, a cloud so fat it briefly obscured the Haze. Buddy's head was plunged into a cyclone of debris. He could barely see his own feet. He didn't know where his friends were. Rhythmic chewing noises came from every direction. From behind bruise-colored clouds came low, heavy chugging sounds, like the panting of a pack of wolves.

"We need to run." Buddy heard himself squeak it.

"What's that sound?" Horace cried. "What's that horrible *sound*?"

Buddy said it louder: "We need to run!"

"Oh, Mother," Sunny muttered. "This sounds bad."

"Those beasts coming," Sugar observed, "are a whole lot bigger than rats."

Buddy shouted it: *"We need to run! Now!"*

From the swirling silt, a yellow paw emerged and steadied Buddy.

"Everyone touch paws!" Sunny ordered. "Follow Buddy!"

Buddy—that was him! So this was the power of Sunny's Teddy Duty: Buddy discovered he could move. In a chain of blue, yellow, pink, green, and gray plush, the five teddies tripped, stumbled, and pitched through the trash. The air grew thicker with swirling garbage as more mountains fell. Grit sprayed the teddies with sandstorm force. Dirty scraps of paper slapped their faces like bat wings. Sunny was yelling something, but all Buddy could hear were avalanches.

Buddy led his friends up an unnatural hill swollen from buried trash. It got the teddies high enough to see above the floating filth.

Another distant tower collapsed. But this time, the trashlands didn't stop shaking. Or that's what Buddy thought until he realized it was things *inside* the trash still moving. He scrubbed dirt from his marble eyes and stared harder.

The Haze beasts had come all at once.

Mice came first, hundreds of hopping gray bodies, enough to gnaw all five teddies to scraps and fight over their Real Silk Hearts. Behind the mice came rats like a greasy black ocean wave, flashing red eyes and yellow teeth. Buddy never would have dared look away from the rats, except for the even larger beasts galloping after them. Razor-teethed possums, sideswiping snakes, lumbering raccoons, hissing skunks.

The teddies didn't move. The Haze beasts were coming too fast. In seconds, they would feel a thousand sharp teeth. So they turned to one another and joined in a forceful five-way hug, the last they'd ever enjoy.

"It was a short life," Buddy cried, "but at least we'll leave it together!"

"Ear to ear," Sunny agreed, holding on tighter.

"Plush to plush," Horace sobbed.

"It's good to end on a snug," Sugar said.

Buddy didn't want to see. He pressed his face into Reginald.

Then the oddest thing happened.

A serene voice spoke from inside Buddy's stuffing.

"U.S. REG. NO PA-385632."

The Voice spoke this nonsense like it was Buddy's name.

"This is not your death, teddy. Not yet. Look up, U.S. REG. NO PA-385632. Look up."

Buddy was panicked and confused, but he looked up.

The mice were racing right past the teddies like a spill of dirty mop water. The rats did the same, whipping the teddies' bodies with their coarse tails. The larger beasts ignored the teddies too, their keen predator eyes widened into the eyes of prey. Buddy began to understand. The mice, rats, possums, snakes, raccoons, and skunks were not attacking.

They were fleeing.

13

The teddies had seen bulldozers in the Store shopping carts, plastic ones with spinning wheels. These dozers were giants. They crept from the green-gray dust, squealing and hissing. They were made of orange metal. They were hunchbacked, with ridged wheels that ripped through the trashlands, flattening items as large as the teddies' oven. The dozers' boldest feature was their mouths: wide-open jaws that gobbled up trash, leaving bare dirt behind.

Buddy counted six dozers. They didn't work in packs like the Haze beasts. Each trundled independently like grazing dragons. They would inhale the teddies like crumbs.

"What do they want?" Sunny asked.

"Nothing," Reginald replied. "Dozers just destroy."

One of the dozers lurched forward. Its mouth-shovel pushed trash so high it blocked out the sun, throwing the teddies into a chilling shadow.

Buddy was still perplexed by the Voice that had called him U.S.

REG. NO PA-385632. But there was no time to figure it out. He pointed his blue paw, stained from the peaches can, at the last dozer to the left. "If we run all the way past that one, we'll be out of their way."

"That's almost all the way to the Haze!" Sunny cried.

Buddy understood why none of them budged. A teddy's natural state was to lie down, curl up, and let someone else protect them.

Horace, the last teddy Buddy expected, pressed close.

"Someone has to run first," Horace whispered.

"I'm too scared," Buddy whispered back.

"I'll do it," Horace said.

If Buddy's eyes could blink in shock, they would.

"Yes, I know," Horace said. "I'm the scaredy-cat. But . . . look at me, Buddy."

For two days and nights, Buddy had tried not to. Now he did. Horace's mint-green plush was in terrible shape, pitted with bare patches from the pizza-box ants.

"No one's going to want me like this," Horace said.

Buddy wanted to say, *No, that's not true!* But Horace hugged Buddy before he had a chance.

"Here I go, friend," Horace whispered. "Or should I say 'boss' like Sunny does?"

"I'm no leader," Buddy insisted.

Horace pulled back. Their eyes clacked together. This close, Buddy could see entire constellations of stars inside Horace's eyes.

"You're going to find out exactly what you are," Horace said.

With that, Horace did the gutsiest thing any of them had ever seen. He scrambled down the hill. What's more, he did so with gales of giddy laughter. It was such an unexpected noise from a teddy that rats bared their yellow teeth and possums hissed—but they also kept away. Horace blundered off into the distance.

"Look at Horace gooooooo!" Sugar squealed.

"He's not going to make it," Reginald observed.

"What does that green goofball think he's doing?" Sunny cried over the dozer roar.

"He's leading," Buddy said. "And he's making it. Come on, everyone! Follow me!"

Buddy started down the hill. A yellow paw held him back.

"If we're going to do this, let's do it right," Sunny said. "Everyone, paws together!"

Touching paws and keeping their eyes on Horace, the four teddies ran as fast as they could. That wasn't fast under the best circumstances, and now they had to navigate Garden E's lumpy terrain as well as the racing Haze beasts. Even bugs fled the dozers now. Buddy felt roaches scurry underfoot while flies, gnats, bees, and wasps pelted his plush.

The teddies' paws drew apart, found one another, lost touch again—but never did they stop. The dozers bore down, huge and orange like six rising suns. But five of them were already behind the teddies. They only had one more dozer to beat.

We might make it! Buddy thought wildly. He wanted to credit that good old ^{TM} magic, but he knew the real reason: Horace. He'd made them believe in themselves.

Buddy promised himself he'd never forget the lesson.

Far ahead, Horace had stopped. He was waving one of his nubby paws. He'd made it beyond the path of the final dozer. How'd he get there so fast? Rising over a dune of kitty litter, Buddy saw the final stretch didn't lead through trash, but rather down one of the cleared paths they'd seen from the mountaintop.

Buddy's silk heart soared. They'd be able to run as fast as teddies could run.

"Almost there!" he shouted. "Run, Furrington Teddies, run!"

He bashed through a jumble of empty baby-food jars and bounded onto the open path. The dozer to his right towered, a giant orange cliff. Its mighty weight cracked the dirt into big, jagged pieces. Oil fumes made Buddy dizzy. He couldn't tell if his friends were behind him or not. The dozer's din blocked out everything.

Except a long, high-pitched shriek.

Buddy stopped. The soft bodies of three teddies piled up behind him. He looked past the dozer and saw a black dagger plunge through the blue sky.

"*Look out, Horace!*" Buddy yelled.

Horace kept waving, ignorant of the descending shadow.

A curved beak stabbed into Horace's chest. Pale stuffing blurted outward. Horace was hurled to the dirt. A second later, his body flew upward. The garbage gull with the scarred face had him. Buddy watched as the gull's wings flapped and Horace was lifted. Higher they flew, higher. Horace's paws and legs dangled limply. His head flopped too, and Buddy saw Horace's eyes staring down at him, a final, terrified goodbye before he vanished into the Haze.

"Nonononono!" Sugar screamed.

A bit of stuffing drifted down like snow.

Buddy's feet felt nailed to the dirt. Horace, a So-So-Soft Furrington Teddy with a Real Silk Heart—gone forever? The Voice who'd called Buddy U.S. REG. NO PA-385632 had promised it wasn't time for Buddy's death . . . but had said nothing about Horace.

"There's more of them," Reginald croaked.

A dozen ruthless birds arrowed downward. Buddy understood why the scarred gull had gotten Horace. The teddies smelled like garbage and blended into the landfill. But here on this open path, they were easy pickings.

"Off the path! Back into the trash!" he shouted.

Buddy pushed Sunny, while Reginald shoved at the screaming Sugar.

The four teddies—only four now!—tumbled back into the garbage. They bashed through rotten lumber and kicked through a bog of soggy receipts. Gulls zoomed overhead, clacking their claws. But the gulls peeled off right and left, because dozers were coming fast. The teddies sprinted for the Haze, directly across the path of the coming dozer.

Sunny shouted, Buddy moaned, and Sugar screamed.

The teddies made it by inches. The dozer swept behind him so close that engine heat ruffled Buddy's tail. The dozer kept on straight, like it had never noticed any teddies in the first place. Buddy's legs shook. They'd made it! Away from the dozers, anyway. Above, the gulls circled.

"What's that?" Buddy said, pointing.

A large black metal bowl was propped up by a chopstick.

"The lid of a backyard grill," Reginald said.

"Who cares what it is!" Sunny snarled. "Get under it!"

They hurried to its black rim and tucked their bodies into the lid's dark cave. Seconds later, gull beaks clanged against it.

Soon, the clanging was replaced by flapping leaves. The gulls were off, chasing after other varmints flushed out by the dozers.

What now? Buddy felt the others packing closer to him. None of them wanted to touch the lid, vibrating from growling dozers.

They'd return soon to plow the teddies flat. Buddy replayed Horace's last words and decided to try to be what the green teddy had suggested: a leader. He had to think of something—quickly, quickly!

Before he could, a voice echoed from under the lid.

"Look at you. How you *run*. Do you really think teddies, with their soft little legs, can outrun anything for long?"

14
.

Rising from beneath a wrinkled bread bag a few feet away was a cherry-red teddy. The teddy's left eye had a jagged white scratch through the center. Buddy wondered what could damage a marble like that. He pictured things he'd seen in the trashlands. Rusty springs protruding from old sofa cushions. The goat-horn prongs of a hammer.

The scratched eye was only the start. The teddy's cherry-red plush looked like it had been scrubbed across brick. It was patchy, bald in spots. The seams beneath each nubby arm were fringed with escaping stuffing. The teddy's entire belly was stained a yucky brown.

When the red teddy stood up, Buddy gasped. The teddy's right leg was gone. The tines of a fork was jabbed into the exposed stuffing. She moved with a swinging limp.

"Staring at my leg, are you?" the red teddy said. "Go ahead. Doesn't matter to old Pookie. Like I said, it does no good for a teddy to run."

The trashlands shook from dozers. Buddy and his friends rolled right out from under the lid. The red teddy, however, kept upright. Sunny frowned at this and struggled to a stand. Buddy knew the yellow teddy liked to be the most athletic teddy around.

"What happened to you?" Sunny asked.

The red teddy chuckled deviously. "What happened to old Pookie? *Everything* happened. Everything your stuffed head can imagine and much more." She hobbled forward. "Come with me, all of you."

Buddy gestured at Sugar. "This teddy's far too upset to go anywhere."

Pookie frowned. "Looks all right to me. Has all four limbs. Head a little smushed, but no one's perfect."

"We just watched a garbage gull carry away our friend Horace!" Buddy cried.

"Is your plan to wait until the gulls come back for the rest of you?" Pookie asked.

Buddy stood beneath the grill lid. "My plan is to find Horace!"

Pookie's low cackle turned into violent coughs. Sprigs of stuffing poofed from her rips.

"I'm sorry," she sputtered, "but you'll never find your friend."

"Teddies are soft," Buddy insisted. "No matter how far he fell, he'll be okay."

Pookie limped close to Buddy. Her eye scratch was a white lightning bolt.

"Do you need old Pookie to describe what has happened to

your friend by now? How the garbage gulls ripped him apart with their beaks and claws? Old Pookie takes no pleasure in passing along bad news. But your friend is gone, blue teddy."

"Why should we believe you?" Sunny barked. "We don't know anything about you."

Pookie approached the yellow teddy, her forkleg clacking.

"I'm the same as you," Pookie said.

"You're *nothing* like us," Sunny countered.

Reginald stood. "She's a Furrington Teddy. She's just . . . damaged."

Pookie cackled again. "I used to think the same way you teddies do. I used to believe being a Furrington mattered out in the big, wide world."

"Have you been out there?" Reginald asked.

"That's how I know running won't help," Pookie said. "I've tried it."

In the distance, dozers honked and snarled. Pookie swiveled on her fork leg and limped away. On the other side of the grill lid, she looked back.

"Come along, come along. Unless you'd prefer to wait for the gulls and dozers?"

Reginald looked at Sunny, who looked at Buddy, who looked at Sugar. The pink teddy still shivered but had stopped screaming.

"Let's go," Sugar said. "This place isn't cozy-wozy at all."

The sun blasted. The dozers had stirred up an incredible stink. The teddies hurried after Pookie. Despite her fork leg, Pookie expertly climbed over an old lawn hose and picked through the stretchy obstacles of cast-off pantyhose. Buddy kept his eyes on Pookie.

"Did you see children out there in the world?" Buddy asked.

"I told you," Pookie said. "I saw everything you can imagine."

"If you're a Furrington," Reginald pressed, "where's your box?"

"I can't possibly recall."

"You must be even older than me," Reginald observed.

"When we got Reginald out of his box, it looked older than ours," Buddy explained.

"If you know what's good for you, blue teddy, you'll stop taking teddies out of boxes," Pookie chuckled. "I used to do the same."

"You've seen other teddy boxes? And didn't help them escape?" Sunny demanded. "You are a nasty, selfish teddy!"

Buddy yanked on Sunny's tail and flailed his paws in a gesture of *be quiet!* Why insult this red teddy while she was helping them? Sunny scowled, slowed her pace, and motioned Buddy and Reginald to fall back with her to talk privately. Sugar was too far to catch, skipping happily behind Pookie.

"Did we all magically forget what happened to Horace?" Sunny hissed. "Why are we wasting valuable time with this red teddy?"

"I'm all turned around," Reginald said. "The dozer noise has me confused. I don't know which way we were headed. Pookie might know."

Sunny thought about this, then checked with Buddy. "What do you think, boss?"

"We should at least see where she's taking us," Buddy replied. "Besides, she might need rescuing too. Just listen—the dozers are getting closer."

Sunny frowned. "I suppose rescuing Pookie *would* fall under a Teddy's Duty."

Buddy clapped his yellow pal on the back. "That's the spirit, Sunny."

"Shh!" Reginald hissed. "Look."

Pookie and Sugar had reached a small clearing in the trash. Buddy sped up to join them.

A white toilet bowl rested on its side. The rectangular back lid was gone, and inside the tank Buddy saw objects Pookie had collected. A spool of thread, maybe used to repair herself. A marshmallow roasting stick, maybe used to ward off Haze beasts. A jumble of wire clothes hangers—who knew what those were for.

Pookie sat inside the toilet bowl with a weary grunt. Her fork scraped the porcelain. Buddy had to admit it was a smart place for a teddy to hide. To protect herself, Pookie only needed to close the toilet bowl lid. "Is old Pookie nasty and selfish for not opening teddy boxes? Judge for yourself, yellow teddy. Here they are."

The red teddy gestured to the left. Now Buddy understood how Pookie used the wire hangers. Dozens had been tangled together to make a circular fence. Sunny rushed toward it.

"Hold on!" she cried. "We'll get you out!"

Buddy followed. But he didn't run. He had a bad feeling about what he would find across the fence. Before he got close enough to see, Sunny held him back with a paw.

"Stop, boss. You don't want to see this."

Buddy was grateful for his friend's protection. But as a leader, it was his job to look.

Inside the wire circle were six black lumps. It took Buddy a moment to realize the lumps used to be boxes. All six had been torched. The contents had been burned to ash. Just enough detail remained for Buddy to know they'd been Furrington Teddy boxes.

15

W elcome," Pookie said, "to the Cemetery of Sorrow."

The four friends gathered at the fence. They were sad and silent. Buddy felt Sugar touch his paw. He was grateful. He reached out and touched Sunny's paw. Sunny reached for Reginald, but Reginald didn't notice. The gray teddy stood alone, staring in disbelief at the gummy black wads that used to be teddies.

"They're with the Mother now," Sugar sniffled. "Nice teddy-weddies."

"You . . . found them like this?" Reginald asked.

"Alas," Pookie replied from afar. "The fence is my silly teddy attempt at respect."

"I don't understand," Buddy said. "Teddies can't hurt anyone. So why would people hurt teddies?"

Pookie's voice reverberated inside the toilet. "Someone out there doesn't like us."

Reginald walked to the toilet and began to climb it. Teddy feet are slippery, so Sunny helped him. Buddy gazed across Garden E. Bad news: Two of the dozers had turned around and now faced the teddies' direction. Hundreds of garbage gulls followed the dozers, feasting on the trash kicked up by the giant wheels.

"We need to get moving," Buddy said.

"The end of the Haze is close," Reginald reported from the top of the toilet.

"What does it look like?" Sunny asked.

"There's a fence. Not like the Cemetery of Sorrow fence. This one is huge and has big, diamond-shaped links."

"Diamonds?" Sugar gasped. "Can I put them on my tiara?"

Buddy jogged to the toilet. "Reginald! Get down! The dozers!"

Sunny reached up to help the gray teddy down. "Okay, boss, what do we do?"

"We get to that fence as fast as we can." Buddy looked at Pookie. "What's out there? What are we going to find? Which way should we go?"

"If I tell you," Pookie said, "I'm afraid you won't give it a try."

Sunny grabbed the red teddy and dragged her out of the bowl. Pookie cried out in shock. Her fork dislodged from her leg, and Pookie fell face-first into a soggy cupcake wrapper.

"Sunny!" Buddy shouted. "What are you doing? Teddies don't fight!"

"We're about to risk our teddy lives out there!" Sunny yelled into Pookie's half-bald face. "You tell us what we need to know!"

"Here's what you need to know: You better hurry." Pookie

smiled. Her scratched eyeball rolled to the side. "Those dozers will be here soon. The gulls will snap you up, just like they did your friend."

"You call yourself a Furrington? Don't you have any sense of Teddy Duty?"

Pookie grinned meanly—but a little sadly too.

"If you want to survive beyond the Haze, teddy," she said, "you have to go a little bad."

Sunny's face pinched in anger. "Why, you little—"

Buddy batted away Sunny's paws. Reginald took the cue and snatched Sunny's left leg. Together they dragged her off Pookie, while Sugar skipped in a circle around them.

Buddy weaseled free from the plush pile and helped Pookie to a sitting position. He brushed cupcake crumbs off her face and tucked some stuffing back into her armpit.

"Don't you *want* to help us?" Buddy asked softly.

With a hiss and roar, the orange head of a dozer crested over the nearest hill. Sunny and Reginald pulled themselves to their feet. But Buddy did not move a thread, not yet.

Pookie trembled.

"I *do* want to help," she whispered. "What happened beyond the Haze . . . it changed old Pookie. It made her a worse teddy. I'm sorry."

Sugar waddled close and stroked Pookie's ragged red head. Her tinfoil tiara winked in the sun.

"Please, Miss Pookie, ma'am. Tell us where to go."

The tiara quit twinkling as the Cemetery of Sorrow was thrown into shadow. The trashlands crackled with a hundred pieces of junk shattering at once: hair dryers, model airplanes, rusted trumpets, punctured basketballs. All of it heaved toward the teddies in a trash tsunami.

The dozers had found them.

16

With her fork gone, Pookie couldn't run by herself. Buddy and Sunny half carried her, each grabbing a red paw. Reginald ran out in front, adjusting Sugar each time the pink teddy veered left or right. All of them ran so fast Buddy worried their legs would snap off and they'd fall into the muck, totally legless—worse off than Pookie.

Hot air blasted from the dozer's engine. Buddy's fabric burned.

"Follow the toothbrushes, teddies!" Pookie cried.

Buddy thought Pookie's head had lost its stuffing until he saw a used blue toothbrush poking from the dirt just ahead. Reginald saw it too and ran for it. When they reached it, they saw a silver toothbrush stabbed into the garbage ten feet off.

Pookie had marked the path to the end of the Haze.

As Buddy ran, he pictured the Pookie of the past: cherry red, velvety soft, smelling of the Store, brimming with optimism. She'd failed to find a child beyond the Haze, and it had turned her bitter.

But with Pookie, there were five Furringtons again. Together they could make it and find a child for each of them.

"Quit daydreaming, boss!" Sunny shouted. "Faster, faster!"

The dozer closed the distance. Just a few teddy lengths away. Garbage from the shovel shot over their heads: scraps of yoga mat, old playing cards, a seat-belt strap, the puffy ball of a stocking cap. Buddy felt trash tumbling against his back. In seconds, they'd be buried.

Reginald and Sugar cut left at a sparkly purple toothbrush. Buddy and Sunny followed, but carrying Pookie was hard. They were lagging behind.

"Listen to me!" Pookie screamed. "I know where to find children! Lots of them! I saw them! They were laughing! They were happy!"

"Where?" Buddy shouted.

"Keep yourselves pointed toward the falling sun! Find the Yellow Plastic Hills! I don't remember the name of the place, but there are children there!"

"Will they forgive us?" Buddy cried. "For what we did to get thrown away?"

"I don't know!" Pookie replied. "When you get there, beware of Mad!"

"Mad?!" Sunny sputtered. "What kind of name is Mad?!"

"She's a Furrington. But she'll try to trick you!"

"Furringtons should all be friends!" Buddy cried. "Haven't *you* become *our* friend, Pookie?"

Pookie twisted her ragged old body with such unexpected force she tore herself free of the teddies' grip. Buddy and Sunny skidded to a halt and looked back.

Behind Pookie, the dozer was the size of the whole world.

"Yes," the red teddy said with a smile. "Old Pookie *is* your friend. Which is why I am going to stop slowing you down. Good luck, teddies."

The dozer's steel jaws slid around Pookie, and the giant ball of trash—like chewed food in an open mouth—rolled over her.

"*Pookie!*" Buddy sobbed.

Sunny shoved him. "It's too late. Run!"

Pookie's sacrifice allowed them to live. They were twice as fast, and by the time Buddy and Sunny rounded the final toothbrush, they'd pulled even with Reginald and Sugar. Their stuffed feet hit concrete. It was too smooth and they were going too fast. They tumbled, four furry balls, until Buddy's muzzle was flattened by something hard.

Gray wire in diamond-shaped links.

They'd reached the fence.

Buddy looked back. The dozer wasn't interested in concrete. It swerved at the border of Garden E and rumbled off in a different direction. The flock of garbage gulls flapped after it. Buddy was startled by how quickly the birds faded away. He faced the sky and examined the colossal cloud of steam over the trashlands.

That was the Haze. And they were outside of it.

Sugar's tiara had survived. She gave it a jaunty angle.

"Where's Pookie?" she asked.

Reginald glanced at Buddy. Buddy shook his head.

"Pookie decided not to come," Reginald told Sugar. "She missed her toilet bowl."

"Oh, it was a lovely bowl," Sugar agreed. "Flushy-wushy."

The chain links clanged. Sunny was shaking the fence with her paws. Buddy gave it a quick inspection. Even standing on one another's shoulders they wouldn't reach the top. Buddy looked both ways. The fence stretched on forever. There were no beasts in sight, nor any people.

"We won't fit through the links," Sunny said. "Not even if we squoosh down."

"Pookie said there was a way," Buddy insisted.

Reginald brushed pebbles from his fur and pointed. "There."

The teddies gathered at a section of fence set off from the rest. It had two hinges.

"It's a gate," Buddy said. "This is where Pookie's toothbrushes led us."

"Locked," Sunny said. "But I bet we can squeeze between the gate and wall."

Buddy believed the yellow teddy was right. All they had to do was push their soft teddy selves through the gap.

Instead, they only stared at it. To wiggle past a locked gate . . . that was wrong. That was breaking rules. That was the kind of thing that got children in trouble.

Buddy wondered what the Voice would say about this. Would the Voice tell Buddy—U.S. REG. NO PA-385632—that death waited for the teddies beyond the fence? Or would it assure him there were plentiful children out there offering Forever Sleep?

The Voice did not speak. This decision was up to the teddies. Buddy thought that, to reach their goals, they'd have to break some rules. He recalled Pookie's warning.

If you want to survive beyond the Haze, teddy, you have to go a little bad.

Buddy stepped to the gate and searched his stuffing for just a little more ™ magic.

"I'll go first," he said.

TO PIECES

17

Right after they escaped, a truck passed. The only vehicles Buddy had seen before were pieces of plastic that fit inside a child's hand. This truck was closer to a dozer—huge, ugly, smelly, and loud. Fast too. It zoomed by with a blur of chrome and a blast of hot air, hurling the teddies to the ground.

A cloud of bad-smelling gray smoke followed the truck. The teddies tried to wave it away. Inside, Buddy felt like crying. Only his role as "boss" kept his emotions from bursting from his Real Silk Heart. Surely the truck had a grown-up inside it. That had to be a good sign. Where there were grown-ups, there must be children.

When the dust cleared, the teddies saw before them a long concrete road that squiggled into the distance like a ribbon. It looked lonely. Buddy surprised himself by smiling. It was amazing too, wasn't it? In Garden E, trash mountains had blocked all views. Out here, the world was endless. That had to mean the possibilities were also endless.

Buddy glanced at Sunny.

"This is going to be some adventure, isn't it?" he asked.

Sunny nodded. "But guess who'll be right beside you?"

"We're going to make it!" Sugar chirped. "I just know it!"

Reginald smirked. "I don't know if I'd go *that* far. But let's give it a go."

The road was tough on teddies. Bits of plush were scraped from their feet. The gang moved to the side of the road, where concrete gave way to gravel. Buddy knew about cigarettes from janitors at the Store, and here cigarette butts sprouted like dirty flowers.

At least cigarettes were soft. Everything else was sharp. Crumpled energy-drink cans. Soda bottle tops. An entire hubcap so sharp-looking the teddies strayed way out into the road to avoid it. Buddy was discouraged. This wasn't much better than the trashlands.

But the hope of the passing truck didn't let Buddy down. After the cement road straightened, he saw something that filled his little body with wonder. Far, far, far in the distance were towers so tall they made trashland mountains look like toy blocks. All four teddies stopped and stared.

They knew they were small, but not *this* small.

"Skyscrapers," Reginald gasped.

"Yowch," Sugar gasped. "Mr. Sky doesn't want to be scraped!"

"It's . . ." Buddy couldn't find the right words.

"Fantastic," Sunny finished. "Stupendous. Stunning."

"You know what Mr. Sky would rather be?" Sugar asked. "Eh? Eh?"

"That's an awful big world we're heading into," Reginald observed.

"True," Sunny said. "But who would've bet four teddies could make it *this* far?"

"Mr. Sky . . ." Sugar geared up for her punch line. ". . . would like to be snugged!"

She searched for praise. Reginald patted her head.

"Reginald," Buddy said. "Are there people in those skyscrapers?"

"Hundreds, I bet," the gray teddy said. "Maybe thousands."

Buddy puffed out his chest proudly. "Some of them *must* be children."

"Probably," Reginald replied. "Remember what Pookie said."

"Yellow Plastic Hills," Buddy recited. "Beware of Mad."

"Before that."

Buddy recited it: "Keep yourself pointed toward the falling sun."

Reginald pointed toward the trashlands. "The sun came up over here. So I bet it falls down over there."

Buddy lifted his paws in a way that felt quite inspirational.

"We're headed the right way, Furringtons!" he cried. "Let's go find us some children!"

"Let's do it for Horace and Pookie!" Sunny cheered.

"Yip-yip!" Sugar added.

"Sorry to interrupt the cheering," Reginald said. "But I'm a tad worried about *that*."

The gray teddy gestured straight ahead. It had been easy enough to follow this road from the trashlands. But here their road crossed another road. After that, another. As hard as Buddy looked, he couldn't see the end of the roads.

The road directly in front of them was the widest road by far. Countless cars, trucks, vans, buses, and motorcycles zoomed across six lanes too quickly for any drivers to notice a few teddies huddled on the ground.

"This is called a 'highway,'" Reginald said. "And I have no idea how we're going to cross it."

18

The outskirts of the city were loud. Garden E hadn't been silent, but at least its sounds had been *natural*—buzzing insects, cawing birds. Here, the monotonous slap of tires, the chug of engines, the burble of radios, and the hiss of electrical wires all melted into a background *whoosh*. If you lived in the skyscrapers, you probably didn't notice it.

Buddy definitely noticed it. He couldn't stop noticing it. How long had they been waiting for the vehicles to stop so they could cross? Minutes, at least. Hours, perhaps. Once far behind them, the sun was now far in front of them.

"A fine start to our adventure," Sunny griped. "Stuck at the first obstacle."

"To get *over*," Sugar said, "we've got to get *under*."

"Sugar, please." Buddy said. "If we could only get to those roads, we might be all right."

Sugar wiggled her pink rear. "We gotta get squirmy-wormy."

"That's nice, Sugar," Reginald said. "If we had fingers, we

might be able to climb up that telephone pole and inch across that wire."

"Not up-up-up!" Sugar laughed. "Down-down-down!"

Sunny turned. "Sugar, you numbskull! Will you please pipe down?!"

Sugar shut up. Her head dipped so far into her soft body that her tinfoil tiara nearly fell off. Sunny looked as angry as she had when she'd shoved Pookie. Had Sunny forgotten her Teddy Duty? He rushed over to help.

But when he got there, his voice caught. He could see down into the ditch next to them. From under the highway poked a metal pipe.

"Reginald," Buddy called. "What's that?"

"That?" Reginald replied. "That's a culvert."

"What's a culvert?"

"It's a pipe that lets water run under a road."

Buddy grinned. He straightened Sugar's tiara.

"Is that what you've been trying to tell us?" he asked.

Sugar nodded and sniffled. "To get *over*, we've got to get *under*."

Buddy lifted his paws in victory. "Furrington Teddies! Prepare to get squirmy-wormy!"

They hoorayed. The teddies were ready!

It turned out, no, they weren't. The ditch to the culvert was steep. They slipped on wet grass and flopped into mud. The culvert itself was round, ridged, and small. It stunk too. No liquid was in the pipe right now, Mother bless, but Reginald said the pipe might probably hold "sewage"—a word he refused to explain.

One by one, they entered, ducking to fit. Brave Sunny went first, followed by Reginald, Sugar, and Buddy. They crept along, inch by smelly inch, and were halfway across when Sunny cried out.

"Everyone stop!"

The echo sounded like twenty Sunnys.

"What's wrong?" Buddy asked.

"It's . . . a dead thing." Sunny shuddered so badly Buddy could see it.

"A rat," Reginald called back. "I think it died in here."

Buddy thought. That sounded unpleasant indeed. But turning around wasn't an option. It would put the teddies right back where they started.

"We have no choice," Buddy said. "Step over it."

"This is the least fun thing a teddy's ever done," Sunny muttered. "Arg! I touched it! I touched a disgusting rat body!"

But Buddy saw the yellow teddy carry on, followed by Reginald.

Sugar was next, and Buddy worried. He didn't know how the pink teddy would handle death. Buddy was the supposed leader here, and *he* barely understood it. Come to think of it, he wasn't sure how death was different from Forever Sleep. Why was one scary and one not?

Did Forever Sleep just have a nicer name?

To Buddy's surprise, Sugar didn't seem to have a reaction to the dead rat. She looked down at it for a few seconds, stepped over it, and stood in place, waiting for Buddy. *Perhaps the rat isn't so awful after all*, Buddy thought. He approached with new confidence.

But it *was* awful. In Garden E, the rats had seemed pure evil, darting about with glaring eyes and snapping teeth. This rat was still and swollen. A pale tongue hung from its open mouth. Its body squirmed with bugs. Buddy realized a rat needed to dart, glare, and chew, just like a teddy needed to nap, cuddle, and have tea parties.

He'd expected to be disgusted. He hadn't expected to be sad.

Buddy stumbled past the rat and leaned against the pipe to collect himself. By his feet lay Sugar's beloved tinfoil tiara. The culvert must have knocked it off. It made him smile a little. Saving Sugar's tiara would make her happy, and that would make him happy too. *I'll be there when you need me*, he thought.

He picked up the tiara and brushed it off. Sugar was still facing away from him. He tapped her on the shoulder and held out the tiara.

"Your tiara got—" Buddy began.

Sugar turned.

Stuffing leaked from two holes in her face. There was no mistaking it.

She'd torn her eyes off.

"Oh, thank you," Sugar said, but her paws couldn't find the tiara, because she was blind.

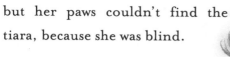

19
.

Buddy was outside, tummy-down in damp ditch grass. It had all happened so fast. He'd screamed. Sugar, horrifyingly, had giggled. Sunny had dashed into the culvert and helped Buddy drag out Sugar, who kept giggling, and giggling, and giggling. The last thing Buddy remembered was Reginald emerging from the pipe carrying Sugar's eyes.

Buddy brought himself to a sitting position. The sun had fallen, and this world's dark wasn't like the trashlands dark. First off, he could still see. Buzzing lights atop tall poles stretched along the highway in lines as straight as the Store's aisles.

"You all right, boss?" Sunny asked. "You fainted on us."

Sunny and Reginald were crouched over Sugar. Buddy got up and joined them. It was a wretched sight. Sugar, already suffering a dented head, now had no eyes.

Sugar was rocking gently, giggling lightly, and whispering.

"What's she saying?" Buddy asked.

Sunny grimaced. "She says she can *see* things."

Reginald held up Sugar's eyes. "I'm pretty sure she can't."

Buddy gasped. The eyes weren't marbles. Sugar's weren't glass marble at all. They'd only *looked* like glass. Why, they were nothing but cheap pieces of plastic.

Buddy felt like he might faint again. Reginald's box had promised, *No teddy is made with more care.* Furrington Teddies ought to be made from the world's best stuff.

Had their own boxes lied to them?

Reginald rolled Sugar's eyes over. The backs had sharp stems. Mother, would the shocks never end? Thankfully, Reginald was perfectly calm, and he showed Buddy and Sunny how the stems had been tied to Sugar's face with thread.

"I'm impressed she got those eyes off with teddy paws," Reginald said. He nodded farther down the ditch. "I bet we can get them to stick back in there. Let me see what I can find."

He waddled away, sifting through overgrown grass. Meanwhile, Sugar kept whispering. Buddy sat close and pet her head. "Sugar? What do you see?"

"Sooooo many things!"

Buddy was alarmed but kept petting. "Why don't you tell me?"

"Stuffing! I see so much stuffing!"

"Stuffing?" Sunny frowned. "Like the stuffing inside us?"

"Swirling like a snowstorm! Somersaulting over streets! Hilling into hills!"

Buddy and Sunny exchanged a look.

"Well, *that* doesn't sound good," Sunny observed.

Sugar went silent and rigid, startling them both. The only part of the pink teddy that moved were the white wisps of stuffing fluttering from her eyeholes.

Suddenly her cries pierced the night like a series of shattered windows. Right away, Buddy knew he'd never forget what she said. It helped that it rhymed.

I see stuffing in a big metal chest.
I see stuffing inside a twisted plastic nest.
I see stuffing piled along a cold gray floor.
I see stuffing in a crowded brown drawer.

"For Mother's sake, that's creepy!" Sunny cried. "Reginald, we need to put those eyes back right away!"

Buddy resumed petting Sugar's dented head. Her damage made her unusual—but it made her unique too. What if Sugar could see pictures of their futures? That would be wonderful if the pictures showed them with loving children. It would be less wonderful if their fates resembled that of the dead rat.

Reginald returned with a pawload of litter people had thrown out car windows. The gray teddy's big idea was to keep Sugar's eyes in place with goggles. He constructed them from two paper cups and a purse strap, but it wouldn't stay in place. Besides, Sugar laughed that it tickled.

The gray teddy changed plans. He'd found two candies labeled *CARAMEL* melted inside their wrappers. They were awfully sticky. He applied the brown goo to the pointy stems of Sugar's eyes and squashed them back into her head. Just to be careful, he peeled some clear packing tape off a cardboard box and taped Sugar's eyes onto her face.

"Oh." Sugar sounded disappointed. "Now I only see the world."

"Tell us if the caramel doesn't hold," Reginald added, "or if the tape starts to sag."

Garden E had been full of rain evidence: brown puddles afloat with chunks of rotten food, greasy water pooled atop dented boxes. But never had they felt rain on their bodies. Now it fell, light but sudden. It made Buddy's plush feel like mud. When it soaked in, it made his stuffing heavy. Buddy groaned. Sunny swatted raindrops like they were bugs. Reginald shivered, then dragged over a box labeled *WINE* for shelter.

Sugar looked up at her friends. Buddy's Real Silk Heart broke. Sugar's pretty, bright eyes were scratched from the culvert. Even worse, they pointed in opposite directions.

But those crooked eyes saw something in the rain the other teddies didn't.

"Raaaaaain!" She spun in a circle, tilting her face to the sky. Raindrops, fatter now, exploded against the packing tape over her eyes. "Oh, boooooy!"

"Sugar, stop that!" Buddy shouted.

"Sugar, get under this box!" Sunny hollered.

"It's like the stars came down to live in my body!" Sugar giggled. "I'm getting bigger and bigger! I'm the whole universe now!"

The three other teddies hesitated at the edge of the box shelter. Buddy, wet and upset, was surprised by the warmness radiating from his damp stuffing. It was a peculiar thought, but right then, Sugar *did* seem like the universe, spinning in infinity, unafraid of the rain—unafraid of anything. Maybe that was the key to survival. Not to push away fear, but turn it into something else.

Buddy dashed out into the rain.

"Boss! What are you doing?"

The rain was cold! Buddy whooped. It was a funny noise, and he laughed.

"I'm getting clean!" he chuckled. "Scrub-a-dub-dub!"

"A-dub-a-bub-a-flub-a-nub!" she agreed.

Sugar danced around Buddy, and he joined in.

Spinning, Buddy glimpsed Sunny's frown. Spinning more, he glimpsed Sunny's shrug.

"I guess it does look kind of fun," the yellow teddy groused.

With a high-pitched squeal, Sunny dashed into the rain, exclaiming at the cold, laughing at the night's absurdity, and dancing in celebration while she scrubbed her dirty fur. Reginald, a quieter teddy, stepped only a few inches into the rain and carefully cleaned his plush.

It was the most fun they ever had.

When Buddy collapsed under the *WINE* box, exhausted and laughing, he had a peculiar thought. When he and his friends got to the Yellow Plastic Hills, found children, and fell into Forever Sleep . . . well, he'd miss these teddies. He'd miss them bad.

20

Buddy kept the teddies to ditches. Icky places to be, ditches. After the rain, the ground was so spongy even lightweight teddy-bear feet produced muddy water. The grass and weeds were tall and beaded with water. Bottles, lipstick cases, and food wrappers were everywhere, though the teddies had yet to see any actual people.

Maybe that was because all the people were trapped inside long, low buildings Reginald called "factories." Surrounded by parked cars like crouched lions, factories lined both sides of the road. They were gray. They were dirty. They rumbled like upset stomachs.

After a while, ditches ended. They just stopped. It was confusing. Were ditches allowed to vanish like that? Didn't the world have rules like the Furrington box did? Buddy smelled his friends close behind him—their plush had turned sour as the sun dried it. He needed to come up with a way to keep moving without being spotted.

Up ahead, Buddy saw a big blue box standing on four metal legs.

"Let's wait until traffic dies down," he said. "When I say so, run under that thing. Got it?"

A few minutes (or hours) later, they did just that. Buddy took the lead, Sunny kept the cockeyed Sugar on a straight path, and slow, steady Reginald brought up the rear. The four collapsed into a shuddering blue-pink-yellow-and-gray pile beneath the metal box.

From the bottom of the pile, Sugar's muffled voice: "Slightly. Less. Snugs. Please."

Carefully they unpiled. After too long in the sun's glare, they were in shadow. Buddy felt his cooked plush begin to cool.

"That was fun," Sunny panted. "I wonder how much more fun we can take."

"Is this our new home?" Sugar's crooked eyes searched the bottom of the box. "It's very blue-y. Very metal-y."

"I think it's where people drop their mail," Reginald said.

"They stuff their boys in here?" Sunny asked. "That doesn't sound fair."

"No, not *male*," Reginald said. "Mail is like . . . letters you write a friend."

"Pen pals!" Sugar gasped.

"Somehow these boxes squirt letters all over the world." Reginald ran a paw along the metal underside. "They must be thaumaturgic too."

"Dear pen pal," Sugar recited happily. "How are you? I am fine."

Buddy had an idea. "Reginald, what if we crawled into this box? Could it mail us directly to the Yellow Plastic Hills?"

"Better yet," Sunny said, "could it mail us straight back to the Store?"

"I hope you are having many funny adventures, pen pal," Sugar continued. "My friends and me are having a very funny time on a funny teddy trip."

"Reginald," Buddy said, hushed. "Could it mail us directly to . . . children?"

The gray teddy's reluctant pause supplied the answer: Mail didn't work like that. Buddy's teddy shoulders sank. His stuffing felt like wet clay. Beyond the Haze, nothing was simple. Buddy peered from beneath the mailbox. The area was bright, flat, and empty. He saw no other hiding places.

"We lived in a funny oven and our friend Horace zoomed into the sky with a funny bird," Sugar continued.

Buddy felt a paw on his back.

"I know it looks bleak," Sunny said. "But don't let it get you down. We're closer to children now than we ever were in the trashlands. You got us this far, boss, and I'd bet my Real Silk Heart you'll get us the rest of the way too."

"One of the less-funny times," Sugar continued, "was when a rat was dead and I pulled my eyes off."

Buddy felt another paw.

"We're not going to make it," Reginald said, right on cue. But this time he added, "So why not give it a shot anyway?"

Buddy felt a tightness along his muzzle. How about that? It

was a smile. Reginald's gloomy predictions had an unexpected flip side. If a teddy had nothing to lose, why not risk it all?

Buddy took a fresh look around. He tried to imagine his damp head as light and fluffy, open to new ideas. Soon a route through the chaotic landscape began to make sense. It zigged and zagged like Pookie's toothbrush path.

A broken-down telephone booth. The entrance sign of a creaky motel. A trash bin outside a store with wood nailed over its windows. These were places for big, tall grown-ups. But for small, short teddies, they could be hiding spots. Buddy and his pals could scurry from one point to the next. It would be tiring. It would be frightening. But Buddy thought they could do it.

He stood at the edge of the mailbox shadow and prepared to run. He felt the others get ready behind him. More paws patted his back than he could count.

"Oops, got to go for now, pen pal," Sugar concluded. "Love, Sugar."

21

Buddy's strategy of darting from place to place worked pretty well. One factory had an outdoor bathroom the teddies hid behind; it stunk. Later, they hid behind a rusty drum at the edge of a lagoon filled with factory chemicals; Reginald said he could feel the poison at the roots of his plush, and they had to get away.

After a while, factories dwindled, but the Yellow Plastic Hills did not appear. The teddies began to discover other lonely buildings. They gathered behind a ramshackle urgent-care doctor's office that smelled like the Band-Aids kids used to wear in the Store. They huddled under the eaves of giant storage facilities, inside which Buddy thought he heard ghostly moans—maybe some other kind of thaumaturgic toy delayed from a Forever Sleep.

After that came office buildings. They were like factories, only smaller. The air was less toxic, and there were fewer barbed-wire fences. But office buildings felt just as unfriendly. The worst thing was how they all looked the same. Buddy thought the teddies were walking in circles until Reginald pointed out the different words on each door.

TechniSys. IndustraHub. DigiLogistics. HumanoCorp. PharmaServe. Lab-Matics.

"Those are their name tags," Reginald said.

"I hate to say this," Sunny said, "but those are just terrible names."

Buddy recalled the declaration on the front of the Furrington box: *I have my own name!* It had been a while since he'd looked at his own tag. He gathered it from the side of his belly. The tag was crusted with ditch filth. Still it shouted its encouraging: *MY NAME IS BUDDY.*

On impulse, he twisted the tag to see the back of it.

Buddy thought the other side was coated in coffee grounds at first. But it was letters and numbers as teeny as those on the bottom of a Furrington box. These were the sorts of words the people who'd invented TechniSys and IndustraHub might have invented.

ALL NEW MATERIAL
U.S. REG. NO. PA-385632
CONTENT: POLYESTER FIBERS, PLASTIC PELLETS
U.S./CANADA (1-800-555-4369)
MADE IN AMERICA
SURFACE WASHABLE ONLY. AIR DRY.

"Don't look at that stuff," Sunny advised.

"I agree," Reginald said. "Some things aren't meant for teddies."

Buddy, however, couldn't look away, even if reading the words was like rooting around inside his own belly. *U.S. REG. NO PA-385632*—that's what the Voice had called him! It *was* Buddy's name, just a different *kind* of name.

Did Buddy have two sides? Did every teddy?

He was both magical and ordinary—Made in America but Surface Washable.

He had both a Real Silk Heart and Polyester Fibers, Plastic Pellets.

He didn't matter at all. Yet he mattered to his friends, right here, right now.

There was nothing inspiring about this stretch of road or these anonymous office buildings. Yet Buddy felt inspired. He'd never give up. Whether it was because of Polyester Fibers, Plastic Pellets, or a Real Silk Heart, he'd keep moving and talking until he found Forever Sleep for all his friends. Buddy stood tall and used his strongest voice.

"No more traveling during daytime," he announced.

"Whoa, now," Sunny said. "You want to travel at *night*?"

"Silly-willy," Sugar said. "Night is for beddy-bye-bipsy-wipsy."

"Pookie said to follow the falling sun," Sunny sputtered. "How do we do that at night?"

"I've noticed this road heads in the exact direction of the falling sun," Reginald said. "All we have to do is keep following this road."

Buddy pointed. "We did okay for our first two days. But look up ahead. The buildings get thicker. That means more people during the day. More chances to be seen. You're bright yellow, Sunny. Look at Sugar—she's bright pink with a sparkly tiara."

"Why, thank you," Sugar said.

"We'd have to play dead constantly," Buddy continued. "You remember what janitors at the store did to trash they found on the ground?"

"Boop," Sugar said. "Right into Mr. Trash."

"But, Buddy, nighttime is . . ." Sunny looked at the others uncomfortably. "Well, you saw it in Garden E. It's full of . . . night things."

"I know," Buddy sighed. "And it's possible their night noses will smell the caramel behind Sugar's eyes or the trashlands on our feet. Or their night eyes will notice us right off because the world's not exactly full of walking teddies, is it? Or their night ears will hear our little noises and be drawn right to us. Or their night—"

Sunny tapped Buddy's shoulder. "Boss, boss, boss."

"Huh?" Buddy said, startled.

Sunny was chuckling. Reginald was shaking his head in amusement. Sugar, of course, was beaming, just like usual. Buddy realized he'd gone overboard with the bad-luck scenarios. He was embarrassed. But his friends' good humor got him giggling too.

"You've convinced us it's a terrible idea," Sunny chortled. "Let's do it."

22

That night, the teddies continued their search for the Yellow Plastic Hills, where Pookie had promised them they'd find children—and if they were unlucky, the trickster teddy known as Mad. Artificial light illuminated their way. Most often roadside lamps, but sometimes dangling black boxes alternating between red, yellow, and green lights. The teddies were transfixed by the changing colors.

"Let's stop and watch," Sunny said in the red light.

"No," Buddy said when the light turned green. "Let's go."

Stranger lights began to color their way. Yellow, red, and blue light washed down from a sign featuring a hot dog wearing sunglasses. Patterns exploded across a digital screen on a shop selling tacos. Ominous neon in the shape of bottles pulsed from dark establishments that smelled like moldy bread. Buddy felt more misplaced than ever.

They crossed two-lane roads. A lot of them. Each one harrowing enough to make Buddy's legs quake. A teddy couldn't trust roads. They might look empty, only for headlights to leap from the dark like two balls of fire. The teddies were forced to sprint across every road, and teddies were no good at sprinting.

They saw their first people. They were all grown-ups. Thankfully, they were far away. Some grown-ups exited vehicles before slipping into buildings. Others met on street corners. None of them hugged. It felt dangerous, and Buddy didn't know why.

There were no children at all.

The four teddies didn't speak much. They had grown too scared. Nights were full of growly threats. Whirring, chugging, honking cars made them want to flee into the dark, but they didn't dare stray from the road. From some cars, laughter ripped from rolled-down windows. Laughter, the best sound in the world—yet it filled them with dread.

When people got too close, the teddies hid. They hid inside a coiled-up watering hose tucked into the bushes of a truck-rental business—Buddy kicked Sunny, who was hogging the space. They hid under a lawn mower behind Phil's Bowl-o-Rama—Reginald snapped at Sugar, who kept playing with mower blades. They hid beneath the stairs of Keene & Morris Personal Injury Lawyers— Sunny grumbled how tired she was, how they'd never find the Yellow Plastic Hills.

One bright daytime passed. Maybe two? Buddy couldn't keep track. All he knew was that each night the skyscrapers snuggled into their cloud robes a little larger, and twinkled their window lights a little brighter.

Children were close. They had to be.

It was the start of a fresh night when the teddies climbed from a bin of yard tools outside a place called Scanlon Meats. They started their way down the same road they'd been following since the beginning. They all looked a little like Sugar, malformed by a day spent bent around shovels and rakes.

"Another night," Reginald sighed.

"Dear pen pal," Sugar said miserably. "Won't you please move closer?"

"Where the heck are those stupid yellow hills?" Sunny asked. "We haven't seen a single child yet."

Buddy tried to keep a positive attitude. Didn't anyone care that leaders felt unhappy too? He paused at the edge of yet another two-lane road. He looked briefly one way, then the other, and started across. The others followed, griping and grousing.

"I don't see what good it does to complain," Buddy complained.

"Pookie didn't say it was going to take a month," Sunny crabbed.

"Pookie didn't say it *wouldn't*. Don't criticize her. She made this same journey, and all by herself too."

"I'm starting to wonder if Horace was right."

"What's that supposed to mean?"

"It means maybe we'd be better off if we'd never left the trashlands."

"Dodging dozers all day," Buddy muttered. "Sounds great."

"The dozers would have left eventually and you know it."

"What about your Teddy Duty? Does your duty include rooting around garbage all day?"

"At least we wouldn't be lost!" Sunny cried.

Buddy made it to the opposite sidewalk and gestured backward.

"We're not lost. The trashlands are straight that way if you want to go back."

Sunny reached the curb too.

"What if I did? Are you worried Reginald and Sugar might follow me?"

Teddies don't quarrel, Buddy recalled. He should cool down and apologize. The prospect of splitting up their group was too dismal to imagine. Pookie might have made it to the Yellow Plastic Hills alone, but she'd come back with a fork leg—and no child.

But Buddy was tired and miffed at Sunny for poking at him. Feeling as prickly as Proto, Buddy glared at the yellow teddy as Sugar joined them on the curb.

"Go ahead and try," Buddy challenged. "See which teddies follow which—"

Leader was the next word, but it didn't come.

He saw Reginald in the middle of the road. After making it halfway, he'd stopped. Buddy was dumbfounded. What a dangerous place to be. Why was he standing there?

Reginald lifted one of his gray teddy legs, just barely. A gooey red substance stretched with it.

Chewing gum. A big wad of it. It looked hot, melty, and sticky. Reginald had stepped right into it. He was stuck.

An engine cleared its throat. Two headlights blasted from the darkness.

23

No doubt Garden E's dozers had been larger. But in this bigger, blanker, blacker space, the truck was like the moon, hurtling toward Earth. The wheels bounced like boulders through the truck's own exhaust. Its front grill flashed in the orange highway lamps. It honked like a gull and hissed like a snake. Hot stink waves bent around it.

It was a garbage truck.

The truck might even be heading toward the trashlands. How grimly fitting, Buddy thought, that after Reginald got squashed into the tire treads, he might end up back at the Cemetery of Sorrow.

The truck came fast. Buddy's fluffy teddy brain told him to stay on the sidewalk and watch helplessly as the garbage truck rumbled toward Reginald and his gummed foot. But Buddy's Real Silk Heart was a different matter. He believed he heard it rustle in his stuffing—whispered reminders in a soft, fabric language that Buddy had given up being a watcher the instant he'd left Garden E.

Buddy ran. Down the sidewalk, over the curb, onto the road.

"Boss! You numbskull!" Sunny shouted. "Don't!"

"Wheeeee!" Sugar cried. "Look at the blue teddy zoom!"

Buddy hit Reginald at full speed. They smashed together. Buddy thought he felt his Real Silk Heart crash against Reginald's: *thump-thump*. Or maybe it was just the garbage truck's wheels: *THUMPATHUMPATHUMPA—*

Using all of his pipsqueak weight, Buddy yanked on Reginald. He saw the chewing gum stretch from the gray teddy's foot. It would break. It had to break. He knew an instant of hope, a thing thinner and more rubbery than the gum.

When the gum snapped back in place, reality snapped back too. The truck was seconds away. He and Reginald were finished. They'd had one shot to escape Garden E. One shot to find children at the Yellow Plastic Hills. All of it ruined by a stupid wad of chewing gum.

Reginald's eyes clacked against Buddy's.

"Run," the gray teddy insisted.

Buddy stomped a foot into the chewing gum so he was stuck too.

"We started together," Buddy said. "We'll end together."

Reginald nodded, like he'd anticipated this reply.

They embraced as tightly as two teddies could, and the garbage truck ran over them.

The world went tornado black.

Buddy felt destroyed. He felt flattened. Here was the strange part. At the same time, the garbage truck's hellish heat made him aware of his itty bittiest parts. The stitches beneath his arms, burning. His plastic nose, hot as liquid tar. The Polyester Fibers and Plastic Pellets of his body, warm as stoked charcoal.

He was peeled from the earth. He was soaring.

At that instant, the Voice came back.

"Is *this* death, U.S. REG. NO PA-385632?" it asked. "Or is this simply knowledge?"

24.

Buddy glimpsed a ball of gray fluff spin by—Reginald. He and Reginald hadn't been hit by the garbage truck. The rumbling machine had passed right over their short teddy heads. But its speed had ripped them free of the sticky gum and catapulted them into the air.

It wasn't a direct flight. It took a while before Buddy crashed down. He hit hard, as if flung by an angry child, but that was all right. Teddies were good at falling.

He rolled, and rolled, and rolled over what felt like gravel. This was less all right. He heard the *ping-ping* of threads snapping. Puffs of plush popped free, a series of painful burps.

Buddy came to rest at last. He lay there, facedown in rocks. He tried to picture the other teddies, but all he could manage were blotches of yellow, pink, and gray.

He was pretty sure a long time passed before he heard the scuffling of little legs.

"Ahoy!" Sunny's voice. "There's our brave boy!"

Sugar's voice was dubious. "I thought Buddy was bluesy-woozy."

"He's just coated with dust," Sunny explained.

Sugar still wasn't buying it. "He looks like a wrinkled old rag."

"Shh," Sunny scolded.

Buddy managed to lift his face. Yes, those were his friends, all right.

"I'm okay?" It came out like a question.

Sunny kneeled and started dislodging gravel from Buddy's plush. Each piece cracked down like a broken bone.

"I'm afraid you might make it, boss," she said.

"You fleeeeew!" Sugar made rings like an airplane. "Just like Horace! Except you crash-landed, boom, bang, smash!"

Had he? Buddy smiled. How many teddies could say they'd flown?

Sunny helped him stand so she could swat away the road dust. Smack by smack, Buddy's fur turned blue again. Meanwhile, Sugar hopped up and down, awaiting her snug. Sunny leaned close to Buddy's ear.

"Staying on the road with Reginald," she whispered. "That was something."

"No, it wasn't," Buddy said. A good leader should be humble. Sunny pinched Buddy.

"Ouch! What gives?"

"Don't say it was nothing," Sunny reprimanded. "I doubt any teddy in teddy history ever did anything so brave. Proto included."

"Oh," Buddy said. "Well. It was my pleasure."

Sugar weaseled in for her snug, and Buddy gave in to it, trying to let his troubles get lost in pink plush. But it was difficult. He and Reginald had been nearly squashed! The Voice had said additional mystifying things about death! He embraced Sugar harder.

"Apologies for the interruption," Reginald said.

The gray teddy had survived his flight too. The big difference was that he looked fine. Aside from discolorations on his feet, the gray teddy remained quite clean. Even those feet might be cleanable, thanks to the info on the back of Buddy's name tag: *SURFACE WASHABLE ONLY.*

Reginald shrugged. "I managed to land in a lovely flower bed over yonder."

Buddy's steps teetered, but he walked over to Reginald.

"Hey!" Sugar shouted. "I wasn't done with my snug!"

"Glad you're okay, pal," Buddy said.

Reginald, though, did not reply likewise, nor did he say thanks. He gave Buddy a careful look.

"Helping me on the road like that . . . the things you're doing, Buddy . . . they're not what teddies were built to do." He shook his head. "It makes me worry we're turning into things we eren't meant to be."

"We're growing and learning," Buddy said. "Won't that make ven better teddies?"

eginald looked conflicted. "I don't know. I keep thinking of said on our boxes: *I'll be there when you need me.* That wasn't a between teddies, Buddy. It was a promise between a teddy and a child. What if we *grow* and *learn* so much, we can't fall into Forever Sleep?"

Sunny stepped between them.

"Back off, Reginald. Our big blue boss here just did something so brave it'll go down in teddy legend. And he didn't land in soft, nice-smelling flowers like you did. How about you give him some time to recover?"

Sunny guided Buddy to a low stone wall encircling a patch of dying flowers. Buddy resisted at first, but his head was still spinning from his flight. So he sat, and the three others sat around him.

"We'll get back to Pookie's road when you feel better," Sunny promised.

"I got robbed of snugs and no one cares," Sugar said.

"I apologize, Buddy," Reginald said. "I'm just trying to figure things out."

"It's okay," Buddy replied. "That's what we're all trying to do."

Reginald glanced up at the moon.

"As long as we're resting . . . ," he said. "I have another Proto story that might help."

"Eeeee! A story!" Sugar squealed, same as last time.

Sunny clapped. "Now there's an idea! But will you please give it have a happy ending?"

Reginald shrugged. "I won't know how it ends until I get there."

"We'll risk it," Buddy said gratefully. "Start talking."

25.

ONCE UPON A dream and far away, Proto was playing Teddy Poker with the Mother and the eight Originals: Geoffrey, Jasmine, Ulric, Anita, Edmund, Beatrix, Antwan, and Sheila. Of all the games they played, Teddy Poker was the funnest. Even a teddy like you could understand the rules. The only cards you use are the ones with hearts on them, passed around like valentines until everyone feels so loved they start hugging.

Normally, Proto enjoyed Teddy Poker more than anyone. Mostly because he loved to cheat. For example, one time Ulric gave him a queen of hearts. That's pretty special! But Proto had been hiding a king of hearts under his rear end and gave it to Ulric in return.

Everyone won in Teddy Poker, but Proto liked to win *the most*.

The Mother was tired of it. While the other teddies gathered cards for another round, she tugged Proto aside.

"Listen here, Proto," the Mother said. "You have to give the others a chance."

Proto scoffed. "They don't mind. They know I'm the best player."

"You're the best player because you cheat."

"Balderdash! This is slander!"

"If I catch you cheating one more time, you can't play anymore. Understood?"

You can imagine how Proto took this. My, how he stewed, and stewed, and stewed. He thought back to when he was the only teddy around. He and the Mother used to have so much fun! These new teddies had come to annoy him.

As they'd gotten older, the Originals had started to copy Proto's personality. It was like having younger siblings imitating him. Each time an Original did something the Mother complimented, Proto thought he'd burst. Because he'd done it first! A long time ago! Couldn't the Mother tell any of them apart?

He began to think she couldn't. After all, the Mother was old. Her glasses got thicker all the time. The teddies all shared the same white hue as the Softest Fabric in the World. Proto concluded that their name tags weren't enough. They needed to be *distinguishable*. That way, the Mother would again recognize Proto as the best teddy of all.

One day, while drying dishes as the Mother washed in her robe and fuzzy-wuzzy slippers, he sighed dramatically.

"Don't you wish the teddies were different colors?"

"Different colors?" the Mother repeated. "Whatever for?"

"To tell us apart more easily, of course."

"Proto." She shook her dishrag at him. "I know my own teddies."

"Of course you do! You are extremely smart and exceedingly observant!" He dried a dessert spoon before continuing. "On the other hand . . . do you remember snapping at Jasmine the other day?"

"I sure do. I said, 'Jasmine, get your muzzle out of that cookie jar!' Teddies don't eat cookies."

"She deserved it!" Proto agreed, even though he'd rooted through that cookie jar a hundred times. "It's just that . . . oh, maybe I shouldn't mention it."

"Proto," the Mother scolded. "You know I don't care for secrets."

Proto held the dish towel like a baby blanket so he'd look even cuter.

"It's just that . . . it wasn't Jasmine," he said. "It was Anita."

The Mother stopped washing. "Was it? Why didn't you say something?"

"You always say it's not kind to tattle." This was true; she did.

"Hmm," the Mother said. "I'll have to apologize to Jasmine."

"Oh, that's not necessary. But imagine if Jasmine was, say, magenta. And if Anita was, I don't know, chartreuse. Then you'd be able to tell who was who from way across the house." He lowered his voice. "Let's face it—your eyesight isn't getting any better."

The Mother squinted at Proto. She'd been tricked by this teddy before.

Proto kept going. He reminded the Mother of all the mistakes she'd made because of the teddies' identical white fur.

If Sheila were auburn, the Mother could tell when she mummified herself in toilet paper again.

If Edmund were azure, the Mother wouldn't step on him when he napped on the white kitchen tile.

If Beatrix were scarlet, the Mother would stop framing her out of family photos in the snow.

If Ulric were ocher, the Mother would quit shelving him alongside bags of sugar.

If Antwan were verdigris, she wouldn't keep pitching him into her pile of laundry whites.

If Geoffrey were tangerine, he'd look like one of the vegetables he liked to carry to the table—and that'd just be really cute!

Eventually the Mother felt bad enough about her blunders to relent. She informed the teddies of her decision over brunch.

"After brunch," she announced, "we're going to have a spa day."

The Originals rattled their silverware and did the teddy dance.

When they were done, Anita asked, "What's a spa day?"

If any teddy was getting too savvy, it was Anita. Proto would have to keep an eye on Anita.

"You'll all get baths in alphabetical order," the Mother said, "and then I'll dye you."

"Die?!" Anita gasped, clutching her soft head.

Proto wished hard for Anita to go away.

"No, *dye*," the Mother sighed. "It means you're all going to be pretty colors."

The Mother was true to her word. After the teddies cleared brunch, she took the first teddy alphabetically—doubtful Anita—and carried her into her sewing room.

One by one, Proto watched the Originals receive the bold new colors he'd suggested: Anita was chartreuse, Antwan was verdigris, Beatrix was scarlet, and so on. Although he was not last alphabetically, Proto made sure he was the final teddy to be dyed. He loved making a big show.

He strolled into the sewing room like he was king, and when the Mother sat him on the sewing table, he crossed his legs merrily. He was certain she'd saved the most magnificent color for him.

"Let's really wow them." He stroked his plush cheeks. "What do you think? Goldenrod? Aquamarine?"

"Hmm. I'm not sure those are your colors, Proto."

"Marengo? Burnt sienna? Taupe?"

"That's not what I was thinking."

"Russet? Cerulean? Amaranth? Sinopia? Skobeloff? Feldgrau?"

"Shh," the Mother said. She began to sing a lullaby, and although Proto didn't want to nap, he did. After all, it had been a busy day.

When Proto woke up, he demanded a mirror. The Mother made him ask more politely. He did, and she held up a shiny mirror with a silver frame. Proto looked, wiped off his marble eyes, and looked again.

"Is that . . . is that . . . ?"

"It's blue," the Mother said.

"Blue?" Proto looked up at her. "You dyed me blue?"

"A very handsome blue," she said.

"Out of all the spectacular colors . . . you choose *blue*?"

The Mother winked over the top of the mirror.

"Sometimes the simplest things are the best," she said.

Proto did feel better after the Mother presented him to the Originals. They didn't think his blue was boring at all. Not only did they do the teddy dance, they did the teddy shuffle, the teddy mamba, and the teddy salsa as well.

"I have one more surprise," the Mother said. "While you were napping, each of you underwent a minor surgery."

A bombination rose among the teddies.

"Surgery?" asked Edmund.

"Are we sick?" pressed Geoffrey.

"Did we die from dye?" cried Anita.

The Mother folded her old, friendly hands.

"Inside every one of you," she said, "is a heart."

The teddies stared in awe at their own bellies.

"I came up with the idea seeing all those hearts in Teddy Poker." She raised an eyebrow at Proto. "Specifically, when I caught one of you hiding a few cards under his bottom."

Proto's plush felt hot. He was ashamed.

"That's when I realized *hiding* a heart could make it even more powerful."

Proto felt the heat of shame change to a glow of pride.

Only one thing bothered him. While the other teddies celebrated,

the Mother turned away and wiped her face. Proto believed she was crying. Why on earth, after such a success, would she be sad?

He found out soon.

One day, a friend of the Mother's came over for cookies and tea. The Mother had warned Proto and the Originals not to talk or move in front of other people. Other people wouldn't understand teddies as special as them. But this particular guest had brought a smaller person with her—a little girl. The teddies had never seen a little girl up close and were curious.

But they played dead as instructed. When the girl saw the teddies, however, she made a noise unlike any they'd ever heard. It was a scream, but instead of terrifying Proto, it electrified him with joy. The little girl ran back to her mother and tugged on her arm.

"My little girl wants one of those teddies very badly," the woman said. "They're so colorful!"

Proto was alarmed to see the Mother dabbing her eyes again.

"I know," the Mother replied. "Once I dyed them, I knew people would ask."

The Mother sniffled and kept talking. She gestured at the leaky sink, the cracked window repaired with tape. The woman pulled money from her purse. The Mother took it and gestured at the pile of teddies.

By this point, Proto had hidden behind the magazine rack. Whatever was going on, he wanted no part of it.

The little girl hoorayed and scrambled toward the teddies. Being a teddy himself, Proto noticed the tiny little motions of all the Originals seizing in suspense.

The girl swept Anita into her arms and hugged her.

Anita looked happier than any teddy Proto had ever seen. And then, like a light switching off, Anita was gone. Only her teddy body remained, as lifeless as a pillow. The little girl sure didn't notice. She was still happily blabbering to the chartreuse teddy as she and the woman left the house.

Proto never saw Anita again.

He thought he might feel good about it.

But he did not feel good about it. Maybe it was because the other Originals were no longer the same. They lost interest in Teddy Poker. They didn't show up for Proto's teddy picnics. They spent hours gazing sadly out windows, perking up only when they spotted children. Proto sensed a new desire radiating from their hidden hearts.

They wanted what Anita had.

Proto stayed hidden as, one by one, the Originals got what they wanted. A plumber spotted Sheila and told the Mother he'd fix the toilet for free if he could have the auburn teddy. A census worker noticed Jasmine, whipped out a checkbook, and walked away with the magenta teddy. A pizza delivery girl saw Beatrix and said she loved her, and the Mother was so touched she gave her the scarlet teddy as a tip.

And on and on, each teddy's spirit slipping away the instant they were hugged.

Soon, there were no teddies left but Proto.

He'd wanted teddy friends, and he'd gotten them. He'd wanted them all to be different, and he'd gotten that too. He'd even wanted Anita to be gone, and now the Originals were all gone. *His friends were all gone.*

He walked up to the Mother, who was getting ready for bed.

"When you put in our Real Silk Hearts," Proto guessed, "you did something else too."

The Mother smiled gently. "You've always been a clever teddy."

"You made it so if anyone else hugs us, we stop walking and talking."

"I call it Forever Sleep. Other people in the world—they wouldn't understand, Proto. It's better this way." She sat on the bed. "Just you and me now, old friend."

"How wonderful," Proto lied.

"Just like the old days," the Mother said.

"I'm so happy," Proto lied.

The Mother held out her arms.

"You silly teddy," she said.

She didn't remind Proto she'd warned him about all this. She was kinder than that. Instead, she picked up the blue teddy—her favorite teddy, after all—and hugged him. He hugged back, harder and harder, until he felt, deep inside his stuffing, the throb of his new silk heart.

26
•

The only sound was the traffic, a block or two away on Pookie's road.

"Poor Mr. Proto," Sugar said at last. "He didn't get Forever Sleep."

"He didn't seem to *want* Forever Sleep," Buddy added.

Sugar wagged a paw. "That's because he was a troublemaker. Sure, he's fun to hear stories about. But I don't think we're supposed to *act* like him. I think we're supposed to act like the Originals."

"Then why doesn't Reginald know any stories about Anita? Or Geoffrey, or Ulric, or Beatrix?" Buddy asked. "It seems like it'd be a *good* thing to be a teddy people told stories about."

He looked at Reginald. He was worried his gray friend would disagree. After all, it was Reginald who'd asked, *What if we grow and learn so much, we can't fall into Forever Sleep?* Maybe the most vital part of a Teddy's Duty was to stay quiet and still their whole lives, no matter what.

Reginald shrugged. "I don't think we'll know the true answer until the end. Until we fall into Forever Sleep ourselves."

Sunny stood and briskly patted dirt from her tail.

"First we need to find the Yellow Plastic Hills. Everyone ready to hit the road?"

Buddy got up and helped Sugar stand without losing her tiara. He started toward the sidewalk before noticing Reginald hadn't moved. Buddy stopped, followed by Sugar, followed by Sunny.

"I don't think the road is necessary," Reginald said.

"What are you talking about?" Buddy asked.

The gray teddy pointed over his shoulder.

"Correct me if I'm wrong, but isn't that the Store?"

Buddy shaded his plastic eyes and wandered closer. The others followed. Just a little farther down the side road was a big building. How had none of the teddies noticed it? Its lights were blazing white suns compared to the lulling purple moonlight.

Buddy, Reginald, Sunny, and Sugar swayed in awe before it.

Hard, square corners. A broad, flat roof. As windowless as every factory they'd seen, aside from an entrance of translucent glass. Spectral white light flooded from within and made the parking lot glow. Over the entrance, the Store's name shouted in letters the size of trash mountains. Buddy only recognized one of the words, but it was the best word possible:

TOYS

"It's really the Store," Sunny said.

A leader's job was to be careful, Buddy told himself.

"Did any of us ever *see* the outside of the Store?" he asked.

"I'd swear on the Mother's name this is the Store!" Sunny objected. "How many giant buildings with *TOYS* on it can there be?"

Buddy recoiled. "I just didn't expect to find it so soon."

"Pookie was probably too scared to leave the main road. But *we* weren't—no, ma'am! And look what we found! The Store, just waiting for teddies brave enough to find it." Sunny flapped her yellow paws. "What's wrong with you numbskulls? Let's go!"

Sunny scampered away, up the center of the lot.

Buddy looked at Reginald, who shrugged.

"It does say *TOYS*," Reginald allowed.

That was good enough for Buddy. He grinned and placed a paw on Sugar's back.

"To the Store! Follow Sunny!"

He didn't care if he was still a little dizzy. He let himself be happy—not just happy, *ecstatic*—and ran as wildly as he could with Sugar right beside him. Here it was! It was as if the metal mailbox they'd found had, in fact, mailed them to their destination. Soon Buddy could stop living this hard life and, just like the Originals, give in to Forever Sleep.

"The Store!" Buddy did a cartwheel. He knew how to cartwheel?!

"The Stooooore!" Sugar did the teddy dance. She knew the teddy dance?!

Near the Store's front doors, their frolicking bodies tumbled into Sunny. The yellow teddy chuckled at their antics, though she looked mystified.

"Can't find a way in," she admitted.

"Make the doors do the zoop!" Sugar cried. "The zoop-boop-de-oop!"

Buddy giggled. "That's right! The doors are supposed to, well, *zoop* right open when you get close. What a palace of ™ magic!"

Sunny did a half-hearted jig in front of the doors. "Zoop? Uh, zoop?"

"Store's closed," Reginald called.

Buddy, Sunny, and Sugar looked right. Past the bright, purring capsule of the soda machine and the eerie glow of the movie-disc dispenser, Reginald stood alone. His polite voice carried out here, away from the noisy main road.

"But the lights are on!" Buddy sputtered. "Just look! I see fancy silver carts! Big, buttony registers! And candy! Candy's for children! Reginald, there's going to be *children* in there come morning!"

Sugar struck a pose. "My tiara's gonna look fierce in there, y'all," she said to no one.

"If you're right, Buddy, we better get on those shelves right away," Reginald said.

"The gray guy's got a point," Sunny said.

Reginald motioned toward the rear of the building. "Maybe there's a door in the back."

It was a longer walk than expected. The parking lot was as vast and black as an ocean. The hum of the long-necked lamps and the chug of the Store's air-conditioning panted like predators. For once, none of it worried Buddy. Every fiber of his stuffing snapped with joy.

Behind the store, a lamp buzzed high atop a pole, spilling orange light upon four dark semi-trailers and two loading ramps. Pretty creepy, but the teddies were too excited to be creeped.

"I see a door!" Buddy cried.

"Darn tooting you do!" Sunny whooped.

"It's a big door too!" Reginald enthused.

"Doors rhymes with snores!" Sugar contributed.

"And floors and wars and boars and roars!" Buddy laughed, pulling the pink teddy in for a snug. "Let's go, teddies!"

With Buddy in the lead, they scrambled and tumbled like the carefree kittens they'd spotted a few days ago, right through the center of the darkness.

Buddy herded the laughing teddies toward the building's shadowed edge. There, Reginald took over, leading them up the loading ramp. The concrete was gluey with old gasoline and stunk like tire rubber—but who cared? They all saw the teddy-sized gap at the bottom of the loading door. They looked at one another, grinned, and nodded.

They would be in children's arms lickety-split.

27

U nusual shapes pressed from the gloom like monsters hiding behind black curtains. Machines clicked, whirred, and beeped, and red charger lights smoldered like the raccoon eyes they'd seen staring from alleyways. Buddy wondered if they should be scared.

But how could they be? This was the Store! No teddy could be careful at a time like this! The foursome hustled for the only objective they saw, a strip of bluish light. The blue grew until they came upon a whole room lit from above by long, tubular bulbs. It was still pretty dark. The greenish cement floor absorbed most of the light.

Dividing the room were ranks of rusty shelving units.

"Shelves!" Sunny cried. "Can you believe it, boss?"

Buddy grinned, dodged the joyfully hopping Sugar, and stared upward. The first set of shelves held an amazing variety of toys, from plastic dinosaurs and paint sets, to building blocks and handheld video games. None of it was arranged as nicely as Buddy remembered. The toys were just piled there.

"We'll get to the pretty part soon," Buddy promised the others. "I bet this is where they keep toys they haven't put on sale yet."

"Or toys no one wanted," Reginald said.

Buddy hadn't considered this. There were clear signs these products weren't popular. Many were dented like Sugar's head. Most were dusty. Piles of flattened cardboard packaging were everywhere. Box cutters lay all over, sharp and shining. The floor was littered with jagged hunks of packing foam and scraps of bubble wrap.

Huge garbage bins waited quietly.

Sunny's yellow paws slapped down, one on Buddy's shoulder, one on Reginald's.

"Why does your stitching look so worried?" Sunny laughed. "This is some sort of stockroom. So what? The sale shelves are close! Let's find them!"

Buddy grinned. Sunny was right.

"Almost there, teddies!" he shouted. "We'll be seeing children soon!"

The four friends hip-hoorayed and scurried. So quickly, in fact, they kept bumping into one another. Their fuzzy bodies began to generate static electricity. This never happened outdoors. It smarted! But it was also hilarious.

Snap!

"Eeeps!" Sugar yelped. "That tickled my tailsy-wailsy."

Zing!

"Jeepers!" Buddy cried. "My ears!"

Pop!

"Yowie," Reginald cried. "My tummy!"

Zap!

"Whoa!" Sunny belted. "Whoa, Mother!"

Buddy chuckled. "Spread out a little, before we all get fried."

By the time they'd passed the shelves, Buddy had seen robots, instruments, bubble bath, tractors, stickers, storybooks, lunch boxes, trains, plastic phones, dollhouses, board games, hairbrushes, jets, skateboards, fire engines, spaceships, horses, sand shovels, kites, colored clay, and puppets.

But no Furringtons. The good news kept coming!

Buddy hoped the end of the room would provide a clear path to the sale shelves. Instead, they found a desk. The teddies stopped. The static electricity died down. The desk had a hard, straight chair that didn't look any fun. Hanging off the edge were boring-looking papers filled with boring-looking numbers. Also poking into sight were pens in the exasperating color of black. Off to the side sat a white mug filled with dirt-smelling liquid.

Above the desk was a bulletin board. Pinned to it were the planet's most boring-looking papers. One thing, however, stood out. Partially hidden behind other papers was one titled *MEMO*.

Below that word, in smaller letters: *FURRINGTON*.

Below that, a black-and-white photo of a Furrington Teddy in its box.

"Teddies," Buddy gasped. "Look! Look! Look!"

Sugar squeaked. "It's us!"

"They've been waiting for us!" Sunny said.

Only Reginald sounded leery. "Maybe we should climb the desk and read the rest."

Indeed, several other sentences followed, too small to read from the floor.

"What a waste of time!" Sunny objected. "We're important here! Why else would they pin our picture on the wall! Do you see pictures of *other* toys on the walls?"

Sunny's glee crackled along Buddy's plush like more static electricity. Sugar's elated bouncing had the same effect. It felt so good to have their picture on the Store's wall. It felt so good to be wanted again.

But Buddy couldn't ignore Reginald. When the gray teddy worried, it was usually for good reason. Buddy didn't want to lose his good mood. But as a leader, he had no choice. He started to ask Reginald what he was worried about—and that's when a bang blasted from the other end of the stockroom.

On teddy instinct, Buddy and Reginald hugged each other hard, as did Sunny and Sugar. Electricity snickled and snackled between them. A second bang rang out, rattly and metallic, and the four teddies mashed together so hard Buddy almost missed Reginald's muffled warning.

"That banging . . . It's the door . . . Someone's unlocking it . . ."

The loading-dock door opened with a witchy screech. Early morning light poured in.

A man's voice boomed: "Somebody here?"

28

A grown-up! Grown-ups loved to pitch things on the floor into garbage bins. The teddies needed to get on the sale shelves right away. Before Buddy could move, a sharp, melodic noise spirited through the room. *Birds*, Buddy thought in panic. Any second, a flock would swoop down the aisle, led by the garbage gull with a scar down its face.

"Only a whistle," Reginald whispered. "The man's whistling."

They might still have time to hide. Buddy picked a direction at random—left—and tried to push the whole group of teddies that way.

"Run," he hissed.

Sugar leaned toward the whistle. "Maybe the man will be happy to see us."

Buddy might have agreed moments ago. Now something felt wrong. The bulletin-board picture of the Furrington Teddy was dark and muddy. What if the *MEMO* was a warning to the Store to watch out for loose Furringtons who'd broken every rule on their boxes?

Whistling, closer. Footsteps, loud and echoing.

The man's shadow spilled like black tar across green concrete.

"Hello?" the man sang. "It's me. The Manager."

Buddy pushed the teddies again, sparking new electricity. "Go! Go!"

Sunny budged, and that was all they needed. The teddies scrambled in the opposite direction of the Manager. Straight ahead was a hallway. Their little legs chugged down it. All four jumped at the jangly crack of keys being dropped atop the desk. They landed in a furry heap, slipped around, clambered up, and kept going.

Right into a wall. Buddy stared in disbelief. True, he didn't have much indoors experience, but what kind of hallway went nowhere? No windows, no doors, no corners leading to other halls. The Manager's whistling was joined by the sound of boring papers shuffled boringly.

"To get *down*," Sugar said, "we've got to get *up*."

"Oh, Mother, not this again," Sunny said.

"She was right about the culvert," Reginald said. "Sugar, do we need to get squirmy-wormy again?"

Sugar shook her head. "We gotta get upsy-pupsy!"

Buddy and Reginald looked up. Halfway up the wall, at the same height as the bulletin board, was a metal door painted red. Why a door was way up there, Buddy had no idea. But if they could get through it, they might hide from the Manager and find their way to the sale shelves.

Upsy-pupsy said it all: A plastic trash can stood beside the wall, and hanging from its handle were two clean garbage bags. Sunny didn't have to be told. She leapt, caught one of the bags, and began shimmying upward. For all their squabbling, Buddy had to admit Sunny looked inspiring—bright yellow, cute as a button, but tough as any garbage gull.

Buddy boosted Sugar onto the second garbage bag and followed behind, while Reginald started up after Sunny.

"We're not going make it," he reminded.

But a short while later, they did. The four teddies piled onto a narrow ledge at the foot of the red door. One slip and a teddy would fall all the way back down. Buddy squatted carefully to investigate the door.

In the stockroom, more locks cracked open.

The red door didn't swing sideways like most doors. It rolled upward like the garage doors Buddy had seen along the road. A little gap, about the size of a teddy paw, had been left at the bottom. Sunny joined Buddy in wedging their paws inside and pushing upward. With a rumble and squeak, the door lifted a few more inches.

The whistling stopped.

"Hey. Somebody back there?"

Footsteps clomped close, past the desk, toward the hall.

Buddy shoved Sugar into the opening with a final snap of static electricity. She wiggled her pink tail and vanished into the darkness. Sunny got through next, her yellow plush quickly disappearing. Reginald and Buddy began to follow.

Glaring lights suddenly poured down from the hallway ceiling. The Manager had arrived, but Buddy was halfway through the red door and couldn't see his face. Buddy saw only rumpled black pants, a short-sleeved button-up white shirt, a stained black tie, and a name tag reiterating his name: *MANAGER*.

"What's going on in here?" the Manager demanded.

By then, Buddy was through. He was glad and relieved, until he discovered there was nothing behind the door, not at all. Just a bottomless pit, and down it he fell.

29

And fell, and fell, and fell, for a million years.

Or one single second.

Teddies are not good at time.

"You silly teddy," someone said. "Why didn't you look where you were going?"

Buddy recognized it right away. It was the Voice, the one he'd heard twice before. Yet Buddy felt no concern. The Voice was calm. He felt calm too. He let the breeze of falling stroke his plush until he felt cozy-wozy.

He tried to turn his body as he fell. It was easy because he had all the time in the world. He paddled his paws in total blackness until his body rolled the right direction.

"I tried to look where I was going," he said into the void.

"Oh?" the voice teased. "Is that right, U.S. REG. NO PA-385632?"

"I guess I didn't look before my first steps in the trashlands either."

"Mm-hm," the Voice agreed. "You *did* stare at your feet a lot back then, didn't you?"

Buddy nodded. Although he could see nothing, he knew the Voice, whatever it was, could see him fine. Silence stretched out. Buddy supposed the Voice was waiting for him to continue his confession. He realized he did, indeed, have other things to confess.

"When I went through the trashlands gate," he said, "I could've thought that through better. Maybe there was a safer place to go."

"It *was* rather impulsive of you, teddy."

"In the culvert," Buddy continued, "I should've gone in front of Sugar so the dead rat didn't scare her. That was stupid."

"Protecting others is hard," the Voice said. "It can mean putting yourself at risk."

"Maybe I shouldn't have tried to save Reginald from that dump truck. If I'd gotten flattened, what good would that have done?" Buddy paused. "But I'm still glad I did."

"It got you here, didn't it?" the Voice asked.

Buddy rolled just enough so he could feel himself falling.

"But where's here?"

"Silly question, U.S. REG. NO PA-385632," the Voice said. "This is home."

Buddy peered into the void. "Home? Is there a child here?"

"Is that what you think home is?"

Buddy nodded. "Home is with a child. Every teddy knows that."

"So you think home is a place where someone *else* is."

152

Buddy nodded again. "Well, yes." He paused. "Am I wrong?"

"It's not my place to say if you're right or wrong, little teddy."

"But a teddy can't exist alone," Buddy insisted. "A teddy all alone . . . why, that's like a teddy falling down this hole. It's sad and lonely."

"Is that how you feel right now? Sad and lonely?"

Buddy thought for a while. It might have been a long while.

"No," he admitted. "But that's because you're here."

"I see," the Voice said. "And who do you think I am?"

Buddy had a feeling this was an important question. He told himself to think carefully. He didn't want to rush his answer, like he'd rushed to search Garden E, rushed to get through the gate, rushed into the culvert, and rushed to stomp his foot in the gum. If this dark, infinite space was his "home," who else might have access to it? He could think of only one being.

"Are you the Mother?" he asked.

Buddy couldn't tell if the Voice sounded impressed or amused.

"Interesting guess," the Voice said mysteriously.

"Whether or not you're the Mother," Buddy asked, "can I ask you a question?"

"It's your home," the Voice said. "You can do whatever you like."

"If we find out why we were thrown in the trash . . . and it's bad . . . I mean, *really* bad . . . and no children will ever want us . . . what then? Will we just keep going like this?"

"Like what?"

"Walking. Talking. Learning."

"Do you want all that to go away? Do you want Forever Sleep?"

"Yes, of course." Buddy thought. "I think I do." He thought more. "Teddies weren't built for this world." He thought more. "We've had some good adventures, though. Even some fun."

"Walking and talking and knowing things," the Voice said, "is harder than Forever Sleep, isn't it?"

Buddy rolled upward so the breeze was off his face. He curled up like it was nap time. All that was missing was someone to hold him.

"It *is* harder," he said softly. "Being alive . . . sometimes you're all on your own."

Buddy felt someone touch him. Was it the breeze? He didn't think so. The touch felt familiar. It caressed his drowsy head. It was gentle and barely disrupted his fall.

"Don't give up yet, teddy," the Voice whispered. "These trials will pass like a grass fire. The stains on your body will lift like soil from a wind-shivered leaf. Your questions will be answered."

Buddy nodded, feeling comforted, and curled more tightly under the caress.

"Time to nap," he murmured.

"No, U.S. REG. NO PA-385632," said the Voice. "Time to wake up."

30

Buddy didn't land with a slap, as he had after the garbage truck, but with a crinkling cushion, like falling on a pile of dry leaves. He was staring upward. He expected to see that he'd fallen for miles and miles. Instead, the red door was just a short shaft away.

His fall couldn't have lasted more than a second.

The red door shrieked open. Hallway light poured into the pit. The light was cleft by the Manager's peering shape.

Buddy held still. Nearby, he felt the stiffening of his friends.

The ceiling lights behind the Manager were too bright for Buddy to see his face. The way the man dodged his head indicated the pit was too dark for him to see the teddies.

"What in the heck?" the Manager mumbled.

He vanished from the opening, and the red door crashed shut.

Buddy sighed in relief. He rolled over to survey his surroundings, but it was tricky. He wasn't on solid ground. He was atop a bed of shredded materials. Some of it was hard like cardboard.

Some was damp, like discarded napkins. As he sat up, the ground shifted and stirred up a smell he knew too well: garbage.

They'd leapt down a trash chute.

"We seem to have a nasty habit of getting thrown away," Reginald said from the dark.

Buddy sighed. "Sugar did warn us, 'To get *down*, we've got to get *up*.'"

"Did I say that?" Sugar piped up. "I am highly intelligent."

Buddy heard garbage rustle vigorously.

"All right, fine, we're in a pickle," Sunny said. "But we're still inside the Store, friends. We're still Furrington Teddies. *Furrington*™—let's not forget the ™. We may have taken a fall here, but nothing can damage the ™ magic in our Real Silk Hearts. We'll prove it as soon as we get back on those sale shelves. We'll do it for the children who need us. It's our Teddy Duty."

Buddy's fear dissolved. If Sunny wasn't giving up, he wouldn't give up either!

He reached out for a So-So-Soft teddy paw to hold. In the dark, he found one.

"Everyone touch paws. We'll need to stick together to get out of here."

He heard each teddy rustling through garbage to find a paw.

"Whose paw am I holding?" Sunny asked.

No one replied.

"Whose paw am *I* holding?" Reginald asked.

No one replied.

"The paw I'm holding," Sugar complained, "isn't holding back very tighty-whitey."

Buddy looked hard at the paw he held. It was difficult to tell in the dark, but the paw looked . . . brown? That didn't make sense. None of his friends were brown. Another thought occurred to him. Why weren't they generating any more static electricity?

The room exploded with the crash of a door being flung open. Jingling noises followed—the Manager's keys. He'd come down to investigate. Next came a series of clucks, as bare light bulbs began to blink on. One next to the trash bin lit up, shedding orange light.

The teddies were in a concrete basement half the size of the stockroom above. More specifically, they were inside the kind of large metal dumpster they'd seen beside factories. The dumpster was filled with refuse. Most of it looked to be cardboard packaging. Sunny, Reginald, and Sugar were there too, half-buried, shocked by the sudden light—and far apart from one another.

All four teddies looked down at the paws they were holding.

They were Furrington paws, all right.

But they weren't connected to Furrington Teddies.

Buddy widened his gaze. Scattered amid gutted packaging were the remains of dozens of Furrington Teddies.

They'd been torn to pieces. Teddy paws and legs were everywhere, fuzzy chunks in countless colors. Teddy heads dotted the terrain, stuffing trailing from their necks. Teddy ears had been sliced off. Teddy mouths had been unthreaded into loose, wild

grins. Limbless teddy torsos were plopped about, name tags still sewed to their sides.

MY NAME IS SCOOBINS.

MY NAME IS IRIS.

MY NAME IS TUFFY.

It was a worse fate than the burnt teddy boxes of Pookie's Cemetery of Sorrow, for there was no mistaking this damage had been done on purpose.

The *MEMO* above the desk wasn't a welcome. It was a warning. If the people of the Store saw any Furrington Teddies, they were supposed to destroy them.

"Mother, no," Sunny choked, dropping a purple paw. "Why?"

"Poor teddy stuffing," Sugar sniffled, staring at a beige teddy head.

Stuffing was all over the dumpster, piled in cottony drifts. It felt familiar to Buddy. But why?

"I see stuffing in a big metal chest," Reginald recited.

Buddy shivered. That's right.

It had been Sugar's first vision after tearing her eyes out.

The Manager's shoe heels cracked across the cellar, sharp as gull beaks into an oven door. The keys he carried sounded like a bag of knives.

"Hide," Buddy said, but too late.

The Manager's head rose over the side of the bin.

The dozers must have been operated by people. The factories and office buildings had likely been full of people. All the vehicles on the road had *definitely* been driven by people—it was obvious from the junk thrown from their windows. Despite all this, Buddy hadn't seen a person up close since his first days at the Store, and clung to a storybook idea of cheerful faces.

The Manager's face wiped out all such notions. Upon seeing the four Furringtons in the dumpster—not torn apart like the rest—his bloodshot eyes went wide inside pale, sweaty skin. He shook with anger until his cheek flesh jiggled.

"What are you *doing* here?" His howl was worse than any Haze beast.

The teddies didn't move. Playing dead was their only hope.

"I don't know how you four got through," the Manager growled, white spit gathering at his purple lips. "But it won't happen again, not on my watch. I'll cut you to pieces, just like the rest!"

31

The Manager rocketed off, his stained black tie flapping behind him. While it was a relief to be rid of that furious face, the hot knots of Buddy's stuffing didn't loosen. This was the worst spot he and his friends had landed in yet. The Manager didn't just want them thrown away. He wanted them shredded.

Buddy's mind felt snarled, topsy-turvy. How could Furrington Teddies have done something bad enough to make a grown-up so furious?

It had to be the *MEMO*. Buddy wanted to explain to the Manager that a teddy couldn't harm anyone, no matter what that paper said. But Sugar's dire vision suggested the Manager would return soon with a single thought on his mind: relieving the teddies of their stuffing.

"Over the edge!" Buddy cried.

He led the way, reaching for the rim of the dumpster. But

the loose trash made it impossible. He ended up sinking deeper. Sunny swam over on her belly and pulled him back to the surface.

From across the cellar, clanging metal—sharp, deadly sounds.

Sunny shoved her muzzle into Buddy's.

"I know I call you 'boss' a lot," she whispered. "Maybe you like it, maybe you don't. And I really don't want to pressure you."

"I appreciate that," Buddy said.

"But we really, really, really, really, really, really need you to be a boss and come up with a way out of this mess. All right?"

"I liked it better when you weren't pressuring me," Buddy said, but rapidly he scanned the dumpster. What was here that could help them? Nothing but scraps of trash.

Well, there was one other thing.

"The teddy parts," he said. "The paws, the legs, the heads, the bodies. Pile them up."

Sunny stared in disbelief. "But, boss . . ."

"These poor teddies never got their Forever Sleep," Buddy said. "Are we going to let their sacrifice go to waste?"

Buddy could see the yellow teddy think: Her forehead plush crimped and her plastic eyes dipped into shadow. But Sunny was a teddy of action. She turned so quickly, scraps of bubble wrap swirled like magician's smoke.

"Reginald! Sugar! Pile those teddy parts! We're going over the top!"

Buddy wasn't surprised to see Reginald already had his paws filled with teddy arms. Buddy might be called "boss," and Sunny might be the boldest, but neither could out-think Reginald.

Buddy began gathering teddy legs. After the first one, it wasn't so terrible. After all, the legs were So-So-Soft and in all sorts of enjoyable colors. If he didn't think about it too hard, it felt like being hugged by a group of new friends.

Sunny rolled a honey-colored torso against the side of the bin, atop which Reginald stacked amber, ruby, and periwinkle paws and Buddy piled navy, sea-foam, and mocha legs. Sugar only contributed one item, but it was one the others had avoided: a teddy head. It was a distinguished rosewood color with plastic eyes still bright and eager.

Sugar stood as tall as she could and placed the head atop the heap. She pet the head's velveteen cheek.

"I'm sorry," Sugar whispered. "Thank you."

Buddy heard a *shunk, shunk!* It was some kind of blades, getting louder, drawing closer.

"Climb, teddies, climb!" he ordered.

Reginald was the first, leaping like a parachutist toy Buddy once saw in the Store—only missing the parachute. Sunny went next, gleefully, like she thought Reginald's drop looked fun. Buddy scaled the pile of dismembered Furringtons to find Sunny standing at the bin's edge.

"Bad news." She gulped. "I think I'm afraid of heights."

"Then let's get lower fast." Buddy took Sunny in a full-body embrace and pitched both of them downward.

Sunny's fearful yelp was blasted silent by a concrete floor. Buddy sprang to his feet and pushed Sunny, whose soft plush glided easily across the floor. Reginald caught on and shoved

Sugar, and the four teddies tucked themselves beneath the dumpster as the Manager rounded the corner.

His roar shook dust from the light bulbs.

"I'm coming, you nasty teddies!"

"Lookie-loo," Sugar said brightly, "there's the—"

Buddy pressed his paw over Sugar's mouth.

"Mmph, bmph, gmph-a-mmph," Sugar concluded.

Buddy only saw the Manager from the waist down. His white button-up shirt had poofed free from his slacks, exposing a joggling white belly. Clutched in his hands was a tool more fearsome than Buddy had pictured: gardening shears, indescribably gigantic, the black blades stained green from pruning. The blades crashed shut once more—*shunk!*—before the Manager leaned into the dumpster.

Buddy fixed his eyes on the only thing he could see: the Manager's shoes. They were old, faded brown, and cracked in a dozen places. Buddy found the shoes unexpectedly sad. Like the dirty bottoms of the teddies' feet, they looked like they'd been through a lot.

For a long time, the shoes didn't budge.

When the Manager spoke, it was neither a whistle nor a scream. His voice sounded like snapping twigs.

"Where did they . . . ? Did I . . . ? What's wrong with . . . ?"

The brown shoes shuffled away from the bin. They stumbled left, then stumbled right, then rolled backward as the Manager lost his balance. He collapsed in a seated position along a wall. For the first time, Buddy could see his whole body.

The Manager curled up like an apple peel. He dropped the shears with a clatter. He folded his arms atop his knees. He buried his face in his elbow. His back began to hitch up and down.

He was crying.

Buddy's plush snapped with static electricity as the others pressed close. He could feel their urge to go to the man—he felt it too. A teddy's most important job was to bring comfort to criers. A teddy's fur, stitching, and stuffing were all designed to absorb tears. But that task was limited to a *child's* crying—those fast, hot, light tears that fell like spring rain.

A grown-up's crying was heavy and cold, and came as if throttled from a washcloth. Buddy couldn't decide if he should feel fear or sympathy.

"Why did you do it, you dumb teddy bears?" the Manager wept. "Why did you do it?"

Buddy felt guilty and didn't even know why.

Eventually, Reginald tapped the other teddies. Once he had their attention, he indicated morning light glowing beneath a door along the basement's far wall. It was a short walk away, and they'd be exposed in the middle of the floor, but Buddy didn't hesitate. The Manager wouldn't be lifting his head anytime soon. Buddy had never felt surer about anything.

The teddies crept out in a wobbly little teddy line. It probably looked cute, Buddy thought, even though he didn't think he'd feel cute ever again.

32

A bright, twinkling morning. Buddy ought to get the teddies to hide. Other grown-ups might react to them the same way as the Manager. But it felt to Buddy like nothing mattered. He'd hoped so hard that Furrington Teddies had been thrown away by accident.

He couldn't believe that any longer.

Back in Garden E, Buddy had understood the dangers of Haze beasts and dozers. Here in the outer world, it seemed like the danger was *teddies*. Buddy tried to think through his misery. Had a tall stack of Furrington Teddy boxes collapsed on people and injured them? Had their plastic eyes fallen off, just like Sugar's, and made children cry?

Those things would be bad. But not bad enough to rip teddies to pieces.

Outside the Store's basement was another ramp. The teddies trudged up it without a word and clustered behind an ashtray. It smelled like the Cemetery of Sorrow.

He felt the gentlest touch. Sugar, as sad as the rest, had snuggled her dented head into his chest. The tape over her eyes crinkled. Her left eye stared at the ground, but the right eye looked straight up at him.

"Don't give up, Buddy," she whispered.

"Why not?" he asked.

She adjusted her tinfoil tiara. "Because I made this tiara all by myself with love and care and what's the point of all that love and care if a little girl or little boy doesn't see it and say, 'That is an extremely beautiful tiara'?"

If Buddy had been angrier, he might have snapped at the pink teddy's silly reasoning. He wasn't angry. He felt empty, like his stuffing had been yanked out. Sugar, though, might have said something wise. What *was* the point?

"Well, *I* can tell you that, Sugar," Buddy said. "That is an extremely beautiful tiara."

"Oh, thank you," Sugar gushed, modeling it.

Just like that, Buddy felt a little better. A few friendly words were all it took. It was a good lesson for a leader. Maybe he could pass it on to the others. He pushed himself away from the ashtray.

"Teddies," he said.

Sunny and Reginald lifted their glum faces.

"That was hard," Buddy said. "Seeing all those teddy parts . . . not finding the sale shelves . . . it was the hardest thing we've done yet. But we've still got each other, teddies. We've still got Pookie's directions. We've still got hope of finding children."

Reginald looked better. "Now that you mention it, I've been thinking. What if there's *lots* of Stores?"

Now Sunny perked up. "What do you mean?"

Reginald shrugged. "It's a big world. Maybe the Store has two different locations. Or three. Or even four."

"Wowie," Sugar said dreamily. "That's a bunch-a-wunch-a toys."

"They may all have the same *MEMO*," Sunny cautioned.

"True." Buddy smiled. "But they may not."

Sunny's soft face squinted over her plastic eyes. Buddy feared the yellow teddy might forget her Teddy Duty again and lash out.

Instead, Sunny's stitching stretched into a grin.

"Good point, boss. Hey, it's getting pretty bright. Time to hide, eh?"

Buddy led the march toward a thin grove of trees. Along the way, he felt multiple paws on his shoulders. It was as if they were lifting him by the plush. Buddy's every step felt stronger. He chose a spot in the trees overlooking the Store's parking lot, and nestled into a shock of weeds to wait out the day.

As the sun inched along the sky, the teddies began to see children. Even from far off, they identified them by the way they moved. Unlike grown-ups, who took the shortest distance between points like trains on tracks, kids hopped and scrambled and scampered, determined to learn what the world was made of by crashing into it.

Buddy, Sunny, and Reginald had to hold down Sugar to prevent her dashing into the lot. As he wrapped his blue paws around her pink body, Buddy felt like he was holding himself back too.

It looked like it'd be so easy to toddle out there, lie down, catch a child's eye, and be swept into their arms—just like the Originals being chosen as Proto watched.

But the Manager's sobbing never quit ringing in Buddy's ears. No parent in this parking lot would let their child pick up a teddy they found on the ground. The teddy might be dirty, infested with fleas, soggy with disease—all reasons to throw them away. Buddy and his friends weren't that bad yet, but they might be soon.

Night fell. The parking lot's meadow of car metal turned back into the still black waters of the night before. Only after the cars left did Buddy stand and brush dirt from his plush. Slowly, the others got up too.

"Come on, gang," Buddy said. "Let's get back to Pookie's road. The Yellow Plastic Hills have to still be out there."

The other teddies agreed this was the wisest course of action. But after taking a few steps, Buddy realized they'd need to pass the spot where Reginald and Buddy had been thrown by the garbage truck.

The memory of it made Buddy's whole body shake. What if it happened again? There was so many globs of spat gum, so many thundering trucks. He found he couldn't move. The others noticed he wasn't with them and looked back.

Buddy looked back helplessly. He felt awful. He was a disappointment. He was a leader unable to lead. The teddies should leave him behind.

Sunny smiled gently.

"You've helped us plenty, boss. Of course we're going to help you now." She glanced at the gray teddy. "What do you think, Reginald? What if we went the other way?"

"It should work," Reginald replied. "We should be able to circle the block and find Pookie's main road again."

"And if we can't?" Buddy asked.

Reginald shrugged. "Then we'll be lost."

Crickets buzzed as heavily as ocean waves.

"We're *already* lost," Sugar said.

Buddy thought it was the truest thing a teddy had ever said.

The four headed away from the main road, but Buddy didn't feel much better. The Polyester Fibers and Plastic Pellets of his head felt replaced with rocks, and his head sank lower and lower. He watched his soiled blue feet pass over candy wrappers and dead bugs.

Sunny's elbow felt surprisingly nice poked into Buddy's side.

"We're not really lost, you know," she whispered.

Buddy looked at her. "We're not?"

Sunny's plush dipped over her plastic eye, a teddy wink.

"It's like you said when we left the Store, boss. We've still got each other. And as long as we have that, we'll always be a little bit found."

33

Reginald had fancy ideas. He theorized if they turned left twice, they'd end up right back at Pookie's main road. It sounded right to Buddy. Well, it sounded smart anyway.

The problem was that teddies are easily distracted. After they turned left at the first road, there were many new things to see. Though the Store was closed, plenty of smaller places remained open, with signs brighter than any the teddies had seen. Sugar gasped at all the colors. They looked fun, even as he had a hunch there was no fun here at all.

CHECKS CASHED PAYDAY ADVANCE
GREGG'S TOBACCO / PHONE CARDS / ATM INSIDE
CUT RATE LIQUORS
GOLD / WATCHES / GUITARS / WE BUY AND SELL GUNS

They seemed like places teddies might get taken to, but only in the arms of nervous children. The kind of places where, if a teddy got left behind, the grown-ups there would dunk her in a trash can without thinking twice. How could such places be so close to the Store? The city never stopped its surprises.

The teddies moved along rusty chain-link fences to rubble left from torn-down buildings. They took their second left, or what Reginald *thought* was a left, only to end up on a block darker than any they'd seen yet. Every lamp bulb looked shattered. Buddy couldn't see the sidewalk but could hear glass objects roll and clink.

"I guess I took a right," Reginald apologized. "Hold on, I can fix this."

They took a left, a real left. On this road, men staggered like they were dead, but the news hadn't reached their bodies. They made wet coughs and slobbery wheezes. The teddies pulled together more tightly. Buddy kept thinking of all the Furrington parts in the Store's dumpster.

The teddies dodged the shamblers and took the first turn they could, another left. A sign proclaimed *PARK*, which sounded delightful. But nasty words were shouted from inside it, and a man was screaming into the sky. The teddies bustled down the block.

One more left turn brought them to a vacant motel that had gone green with weeds. Grasping leaves burst from sidewalks, wall panels, and broken windows. Spots of light glowed from within. They looked like little fires.

"Why are left turns so hard?" Reginald muttered. "No more lefts."

True to his word, he hooked one hard right followed by another. Buddy instantly recognized the traits of Pookie's road.

The shine of the streetlights. The speed of the cars. The skyscrapers, visible again, looming like dinosaurs. It was all good to see, even though it had started to rain.

"We're back," Sunny sighed.

"Dear pen pal," Sugar said. "Sorry it took me so long to write back."

"Yes, we're back on the road," Reginald said. "But I can't tell you *where* on the road. We may have passed the landmark. And we're getting wet fast."

Buddy found himself staring straight up the road.

"The landmark," he said. "You mean the Yellow Plastic Hills?"

The other teddies detected the smile in his voice. Reginald, Sunny, and Sugar looked at him, then followed his gaze to the building just ahead.

From the smell of salt, ketchup, and meat, Buddy knew it was a place where people ate. He waddled through the rain toward it and the others followed. On the outside of the restaurant, a giant plastic sign splashed the whole block in light. It was yellow and shaped like an *M*. Except the points of the *M* were rounded, making it look like two hills—the Yellow Plastic Hills.

The teddies stared in awe.

"I remember that *M* from the Store," Buddy said.

"That's right," Reginald said. "Children ate food with *M* on it."

"*Children.*" Sunny sounded excited. "Oh, Mother. Pookie was right all along."

"Let's go let's go let's go let's go!" Sugar whined.

But the teddies had learned a lesson from the Store's stockroom.

No more dashing in without a thought. Buddy also remembered Pookie's old warning: *Beware of Mad! She'll try to trick you!*

Cars entered and exited the restaurant's lot. The teddies waited for a pause in traffic, then scurried beneath a sign topped with a small version of the Yellow Plastic Hills and the words *WELCOME 24-HOUR DRIVE-THRU*. There, they crouched behind flowers as additional cars swerved by. Buddy wiped his eyes of rainwater and tried to peer through the restaurant windows.

He could see lights inside and what looked like people handing brown bags over a counter. But the moving figures were too tall to be children.

Reginald read his mind. "It's because it's late. Nighttime is grown-up time."

"That's right," Sunny said. "Remember how children didn't show up to the Store until morning?"

"Children will come!" Sugar cried. "Look! There's rides!"

Sure enough, behind rain-spattered glass, Buddy could see a slide, a teeter-totter, and a small merry-go-round, all of them child-sized.

"This is all good news," Reginald allowed. "But we need shelter until morning. No child is going to want a waterlogged teddy."

It was a fair point. Buddy looked around. On the other side of the restaurant's parking lot, near a sign reading *EXIT*, was a green box being ignored by all the people rushing to and from their cars. The box was the size of one of the refrigerators in the trashlands. It was plastic, and looked old and beaten up, but it might keep them dry till morning.

34

Buddy's Real Silk Heart was pounding by the time they got to the green box. The plastic was scuffed, cracked, and dirty. Buddy wasn't so sure he wanted to go inside anymore. But a good leader would get his friends out of the rain.

Right in front was a teddy-sized door. But it was shut with a metal lock. It was also covered in words. Buddy read the largest of them aloud.

"'Clothes and Shoes Donation Center.'"

"What does that mean?" Sunny asked.

"Clothes and shoes," Buddy repeated. "You know, things people wear."

"My spectacular tiara," Sugar noted, "would look nice with spectacular shoes."

"I'd take a raincoat right about now," Sunny said.

Reginald pointed up into the rain. "See that hinge?"

The teddies tilted their heads upward. Raindrops clicked against their plastic eyes. Above the teddy-sized door, far out of reach, was a handled drawer like the one they'd seen on the metal mailbox.

"If you have clothes or shoes you don't need," Reginald explained, "you dump them in that drawer."

Buddy tugged the locked door. "This must be how they unload the clothes."

"And shoes," Sugar reminded.

Buddy walked to the other side of the donation box, right into the full force of the rain. The other teddies followed, bodies curled against a wet wind. The side of the box was in worse shape. The lower edge of the plastic was warped upward like a sneering lip. Here was their way inside. It would be no harder than squeezing their soft bodies through the trashlands gate, the culvert, the

Store's loading-dock door, or the stockroom trash chute. Why, then, did this box feel more haunted?

"All right," Buddy said. "I guess I'll lead the way."

"Let me," Reginald said. "If something happens . . . well, the other teddies need you."

"For crying out loud," Sunny snapped. "I'll go first. I'm getting drenched!"

The yellow teddy squatted to peer beneath the warped plastic.

"What do you see?" Buddy pressed.

"Not sure," Sunny said. "Clothes?"

"And shoes," Sugar reminded.

Sunny ducked her head into the cranny, braced her soft feet against the wet concrete, and drove her fluffy belly forward until she popped through the gap. All Buddy could see was wiggling legs. Seconds later, those vanished too.

Buddy repaid Sunny's courage by not hesitating. He pushed his head into the gap, wriggled through, and felt Reginald and Sugar right behind him. He turned to help them through, and Sunny did the same. Only when all four were inside did they face the inside of the box.

It was dry and dim—but not utterly dark. The green plastic was thin enough to let the light from the restaurant's sign bleed through. It created a sickly green-and-orange aura.

Before them was a hill of clothing three times as tall as a teddy and as slovenly as any Garden E trash mound. Wrinkled dress shirts, inelastic sweatpants, ratty stocking caps, unraveling scarfs, holey mittens, paint-speckled pants, moth-eaten sweaters, thread-bare socks, broken-zippered coats, sweat-tinted polos, stained baby sleepers—and, yes, the occasional worn-out shoe.

The teddies plopped down on the layer of clothes at the foot of the hill. Everything smelled of people, including children, but not in a good way. The odor was sweet and salty. The teddies didn't care. It was soft and dry, and they were tired and wet.

Outside, the storm raged harder. Rain slashed in whooshing waves, drilling the top of the donation box like stones. The whole place shook. Buddy pressed himself deeper into clothing. It was spooky in here and he'd prefer to block it out.

"Uh, Reginald?" Even Sunny sounded nervous.

"Yes?" Reginald's voice was muffled. He'd snuggled deep as well.

"How about one more Proto story? Before the rain stops and we find children?"

Buddy spotted Sugar's tiara as she bounded from a pile of socks.

"Oh, yes, please! A Proto story will make us much less scared!"

Buddy had to chuckle. You could always count on Sugar to tell it like it was. Buddy pulled himself to a sitting position. Sunny did the same. Reginald, meanwhile, gazed up at the ceiling, transfixed by the squiggly gray shadows of streaming rain.

"I believe I have one," he said.

35

ONCE UPON A dream and far away, the sale of Geoffrey, Jasmine, Ulric, Anita, Edmund, Beatrix, Antwan, and Sheila only increased interest in the Mother's teddies. People gushed about the luxurious plush, marveled at the unexpected colors, exclaimed upon learning how each had a heart sewed inside. People wrote, called, and even visited the Mother to beg for teddies of their own.

"I don't know," the Mother confided to Proto. "The idea of making so many teddies makes me tired."

But things were getting bad around the house. The Mother might be a Creator, but being a Creator doesn't pay well.

Her meals, which used to smell deliciously of garlic, basil, cinnamon, anise, cardamom, and oregano, now smelled like the cardboard boxes they came from. The heater broke, and instead of getting it fixed, the Mother put on a ratty sweater and knitted a matching cardigan for Proto. She spent hours on the phone asking for more time to pay bills. When the ceiling sprang a leak, she just put a bucket under it, and all night Proto heard the sad *plunk, plunk, plunk*.

So the Mother decided to make more teddies. If it could help her and Proto live more comfortably, she had to try. Besides, it might bring other people joy.

Soon the home they'd shared for so long was invaded by three women. Proto was annoyed! What about daily teatime? What about Tuesday picnics? The Mother canceled everything to spend time with the women.

The cozy-wozy living room, where he and the Mother had played so many satisfying rounds of Teddy Poker, was filled with long, ugly-wugly tables. The tables were arranged with shears, measuring tape, chalk, pincushions, and needles. The women took positions at these tables beside the Mother. Slowly at first, but soon more efficiently, they made new teddies.

Proto understood the Mother hired these women to help. But he also *didn't* understand. How could anybody but the Mother possess the magic to create teddies?

"Those women don't know what they're doing!" he exploded one night.

"I taught them well, Proto," the Mother said.

"Balderdash! Are they using the Softest Fabric in the World?"

"Exclusively."

"Are they using only the brightest, most beautiful marble eyes?"

"I collected a big jar of them."

"Does every single teddy have a heart inside?"

"Of the purest silk."

He frowned harder. But it's hard for a teddy to stay angry when he's being cuddled. The Mother picked him up, cradled him softly, and carried him to what was now called "the Workroom."

Without the thump of sewing machines, it was eerily quiet. The Mother showed Proto a finished teddy. With the three workers gone, the teddy was free to wave at Proto.

"How do you do?" the teddy greeted.

"Very well," Proto replied. "Thank you for asking."

He had to admit, the teddy looked just as good as Ulric, Edmund, or Sheila. After that, the Mother showed him the bolt of the Softest Fabric in the World—less of it than there used to be, but still pretty thick. Next, she showed him the jar of marble eyes. Finally, the Mother took him to the spot on the table where she stood all day.

There sat a basket of fabric hearts.

They were more stunning than Proto imagined. They weren't just sepia, dandelion, bronze, fuchsia, shamrock. They were also striped, plaid, dotted, starred, glittered. They were printed with animals, cowboys, astronauts, superheroes. They were bordered with tassels, lace, pom-poms, feathers.

"You made all these by yourself?" he asked.

The Mother wiggled fingers bandaged from cuts and pinpricks.

"All right," Proto sighed. "I guess we'll give these women a chance."

Things were nice for a while, once upon a dream and far away.

They did not stay nice. The phone rang around the clock. Men in brown outfits picked up and delivered packages to the house like dogs playing fetch. The heater got fixed, but one of the sewing machines caught on fire and had to be replaced. Two more machines had to be purchased after the Mother hired two more women.

Forget tea parties and picnics! Pretty soon, *nothing* fun ever happened. The Mother worked until she dropped from exhaustion.

Proto tried to convince her to slow down.

"The skin under your eyes is as blue as my fur."

"I need to update my payroll software," the Mother mumbled.

"Your fingers are swollen like hot dogs."

"I need to color-code my spreadsheets," the Mother mumbled.

"You're even starting to repeat teddy names!"

"I need to add my tax ID to my retail license," the Mother mumbled.

That was when the Suit started coming around. Proto didn't know his real name. He wore a lustrous blue-and-white pin-striped suit and shoes so polished they hurt Proto's eyes. After the Mother invited the Suit into the Workroom, he swept off his hat like an old-fashioned gent. Proto found it suspicious.

The Suit's briefcase was shiny too. He pulled papers from it like they were knives.

As far as Proto could tell, the Mother felt the same. She shouted at the Suit and made him leave. Proto toddled into the Workroom to give her a hug. But she was already at her work stool, reaching for a cup of coffee. Coffee! When did the Mother switch from tea?

The Suit returned with his suit, shoes, briefcase, and teeth even shinier. It was days later, maybe months. The Mother looked like she wanted to yell again, but was too tired. When the Suit held out his papers this time, she grabbed them and used them to swat him out of the house. Once he was gone, the Mother flung the papers to the floor.

Later, she got down on her knees and started picking them up.

Proto crept from his hiding place. He wanted to blurt things. Proto was a champion blurter. But the Mother looked too sad. He helped her gather the papers. They were filled with billions of worrisome numbers and words.

"He's from a toy company." The Mother didn't look at Proto.

"Oh?" Proto asked innocently, while inside, his silk heart caught fire.

"He wants to buy my teddies," she said.

"Congratulations." Inside, burning, burning.

"Not just my teddies. My designs. My sewing patterns. My secrets. If I sell them, I won't be allowed to make any more teddies. He'll have the exclusive rights. That's the law."

"Are you going to say yes?" Proto saw flames, smelled smoke.

The Mother lost her balance and fell. Proto froze in shock. The Mother cursed, an awful sound. She sat up and squinted at her hand. One of her old sewing cuts had started bleeding again. She closed her eyes. One tear rolled out of each eye. In the background, the ceiling leaks continued: *plunk, plunk, plunk.*

"We need the money," she said softly. "Plus, maybe he'll do a good job. Maybe he'll make teddies as good as I do, and those teddies will make more children happy than I could ever dream."

Her voice told Proto she didn't believe it.

"Is it okay, Proto?" she asked. "Is it okay for me to sell?"

Proto, who always had something to say, couldn't speak.

"Proto," the Mother sobbed. "Tell me it's okay."

Poor Creator! Proto thought. She'd only ever tried to do the right thing.

Proto thought of all the times he'd tricked the Mother, all the times he made her sad or angry. For once, he would do what *she* wanted. He scurried across the floor, hopped into her lap, and nuzzled his head into her neck.

"It's okay," he whispered. "It's okay."

She squeezed him harder than she had in ages.

"Thank you, Proto. Thank you."

Proto snuggled deeper and told himself everything would be like he said: okay. But he'd just given the Mother his blessing to sell the teddies. That *couldn't* be okay. The wind outside wailed with the betrayal of all the teddies yet to be made. The bolt of fabric struggled, the jar of eyes clattered, and all the lonely hearts flopped like fish in their basket.

36

Lightning lit up the donation box. Thunder trembled it.

Buddy realized all four teddies had drawn close enough to touch.

"I'm sorry," Reginald said. "I didn't know the story was going to be sad."

"It's okay," Buddy said, even though he felt dejected. "I wonder if Proto did the right thing."

"No way," Sunny said. "You don't betray your friends like that. You don't sell them to someone with no love in his heart. No matter what."

"But was Proto friends with the new teddies?" Reginald wondered.

Sunny jutted her yellow chin. Fueled by Teddy Duty, she was defiant.

"Teddies are friends to *all* other teddies."

Buddy smiled but hid it behind a torn belt. He didn't want to embarrass Sunny while she struck such a powerful pose. Instead,

Buddy began arranging the old clothes around him.

"Story time's over, teddies. We might as well make ourselves comfortable for the—"

The donation box shook. More thunder, Buddy thought. Except he didn't hear any thunder. And the shaking kept going, kept going.

Movement caught his eye. He looked up. The hill of clothing was teetering like a trash mountain shoved by a dozer. Bibs, overalls, vests, camisoles, jeans, pajamas, skirts, and gloves slid down. Was the whole thing going to collapse?

Buddy fought free from the old clothing. His friends did the same. Panicked and speechless, they gathered shoulder to shoulder at the edge of the box.

A shape began to rise from the center of the pile. Outlined by the green-and-orange light, it looked like a teddy.

But it kept rising, taller than a teddy.

And rising, taller.

And rising, taller and taller.

"**Teddies**," the thing sighed in a voice of xylophone and gravel.

The thing had a teddy's head. It was the same as theirs. Rounded ears, plastic eyes, stout muzzle. The fur color was a dark, smoky charcoal. The rest of the thing's body, Buddy couldn't make out. The thing was draped in multicolored robes woven from scraps of donated clothing, from pinstripes to paisley, plaid to polka dot, houndstooth to herringbone.

The robes swayed, hiding a body twice as tall as Buddy's. When the thing turned magisterially to gaze down at the teddies, fringes braided from plaid work shirts twisted as if in agony.

Buddy was so afraid he could barely speak.

"Are you . . . are you . . . Mad?"

Mad's midnight head tilted down so slowly Buddy heard the squeak of her stuffing.

"I AM KNOWN BY different NAMES," Mad said.

The teddy's voice was graceful and melodic, but as sinister as a song played on a piano's black keys. It had an eerie echo, like it was many voices, all chanting in unison.

Pookie's voice again: *She'll try to trick you!*

Buddy told himself to speak carefully, very carefully.

"We're Furrington Teddies," he said. "Same as you. I'm Buddy. This is Sunny, Sugar, and Reginald."

He waited for Mad to respond. She only angled her head, her dark eyes gleaming. Her robes brushed over dirty clothes, making ratlike rasps.

Buddy made the friendliest face he could.

"We're terribly sorry to intrude. It's wet outside, and we were trying to stay dry for the children."

Mad's incurious expression didn't change.

"Enough of this." Sunny stepped onto a wad of socks. "Hey! You! Where do you get off acting so high and mighty? This isn't some spectacular castle, you know. It's a box of used clothes. It's not like you have a child and we don't. Unless you've got one hidden under this stinky pile!"

Buddy gave Sunny a grateful nod.

Sunny nodded back, trembling but energized.

Mad kept swishing her long robes, swishing.

"Let's go, teddies," Sunny snapped. "We can get dry somewhere else. Pookie warned us this teddy was no good."

Sunny hopped off the socks toward the warped plastic exit. Sugar dutifully waddled after him, followed by Reginald. Buddy hated to leave the warm box but admired Sunny for showing Mad who was boss. He started toward the wall.

"POOKIE," Mad said in her voice of a hundred voices.

Buddy turned back around.

Mad's charcoal plush had white stitching. It pulled taut as the teddy grinned.

"OH, I REMEMBER POOKIE. **THE** RED TEDDY SO determined To KNOW things."

Mad spread her arms to illustrate the breadth of "things."

Hidden by robes, the arms kept spreading. Not three or four inches long, like teddy arms should be, but six inches, twelve inches, even more. They were like spider legs extending from a sidewalk crack. They were multi-jointed. They flexed in every direction.

Buddy shuddered. He forced himself to think of Pookie, who'd died so they could have a chance at Forever Sleep. Of Proto, who might get in fixes, but never quit hatching plans. Mostly, though,

189

he thought of Horace. Despite being the most frightened teddy, he'd been the one to risk it all. Buddy's last words to Horace had been *I'm no leader.* What had Horace replied?

You're going to find out exactly what you are.

Now was the time.

"*Do* you know things?" Buddy asked.

"THAT I DO, teddy. I KNOW YOu WILL never FIND A CHILD IN that RESTAURANT—not without A GROWN-UP WHO hates you."

It felt like Buddy's stuffing was dissolving into hot tears. What Mad said couldn't be true. Could it? Buddy had been struggling for this goal since before he'd left the trashlands.

He looked at Sunny. Then Reginald. Then Sugar. His friends, each of whom had individual strengths. Now it was like those strengths had been wiped out in a single blow. They looked as flimsy as the used clothing at their feet. Buddy looked back up at Mad.

"But Pookie said . . ."

"I KNOW SOMETHING else TOo."

"But . . . there's nothing else I want to know," Buddy replied.

Mad undulated like a cobra, as if Buddy's voice was a flute.

"OH, BUT THERE is. I KNOW HOW To FIND OUT WHY YOU WERE THROWN AWAY."

Buddy stared. Behind him, one of his friends stirred.

"Maybe it's better if we don't know, Buddy," Reginald whispered.

"Hold on, let's think about this," Sunny said. "If we knew why we were thrown away . . . maybe we could find a way to apologize! To tell children, even their parents, that we didn't mean to do it! It might make all the difference!"

"How could we possibly apologize?" Buddy asked. "We have to play dead in front of people!"

"How am I supposed to know?" Sunny cried back.

"I KNOW," Mad rumbled.

The teddies gazed up at her.

"YOU MUST FIND THE MAN WHO MADE YOU. Prove To HIM YOU ARE good teddies. IF YOU ARE good enough, HE WILL TELL Others."

Now it was Reginald who edged closer.

"The Suit? You know where we can find the Suit?"

White stitching stretched across Mad's dark face.

Buddy thought for a few frightened seconds.

"All right," he said. "Tell us."

Mad laughed, giggled, chortled, and guffawed all at once.

"NOT that EASY, teddy. You give MAD something, MAD gives you something."

Buddy felt a burst of hope.

"We could help tidy your home," he suggested.

He felt the other three teddies huddle closer.

"We could repair your robes," Sunny offered.

"We could scrub out some of the stink," Reginald proposed.

"We could help you try on shoes," Sugar submitted.

"There **iS** ᴏɴʟʏ ONE THING I ᴡᴀɴᴛ."

Her long arms curled inward like two coiling snakes. Her paws nudged under her lapels. Buddy noticed Mad's paws weren't dark gray like her head. One was tiger orange, the other mulberry purple. It terrified Buddy, though he didn't know why. With a sinuous shrug, Mad's robes dropped from her body, and Buddy, who'd seen some bad things in his short life, saw the worst thing yet.

37

Mad wasn't just another Furrington Teddy. She was *many* Furrington Teddies. Her charcoal-colored head looked to be her own. Her torso was the same shade as her head. But everything else—oh, Mother, *everything else*.

Her body had been extended with other teddy parts.

Stitched to Mad's right shoulder was a green teddy paw, stitched to a peach teddy paw, stitched to a teal teddy paw—and on and on, a rippling tentacle of sewn-together paws. Mad's left paw was just as unspeakable, a red-hazel-rose-purple-cobalt-olive-white-silver tube that lashed like a whip.

Her legs were worse because there were four of them. They wormed beneath dirty clothes like tree roots come to life. Buddy felt the other teddies draw away, and knew why. He had a gut fear one of Mad's long legs would spring outward, twist around his teddy tummy, and drag him under the clothes.

Instead, Mad turned slowly, even gracefully, as if modeling a fashion. Unrobed, her every terrible detail became visible. Teddy ears had been attached to her torso like colorful warts. Plastic teddy noses lined her belly like strange tattoos. The back of her head gleamed with seven additional teddy eyes. Ragged sections of plush, peeled from teddy torsos, stretched in her armpits like bat wings.

Attached like feathers to the wings were the name tags of the teddies she'd absorbed. *FRANK, DINO, WILLIE, AL, GUMBO, QUINN, BOOPSIE, SERAFINA, HILDA, ARTURO, POLLY.* Mad's original tag remained on her belly, but it was old and shredded. *MADELINE*, it read, though only the first three letters were clear.

"Do you see," she chuckled, "WHAT MAD wants?"

One of Mad's legs kicked and a sports jersey flopped away. The teddies saw the newest addition of the leg. It was red.

Cherry red.

Buddy pictured Pookie hobbling through the trashlands on a fork leg.

Pookie had sacrificed her leg to learn about the Suit.

"No," Buddy said. "That's not a fair price."

"Not fair?"

Mad's nine eyes flashed in the green-orange light, and her arms flailed, crackling her tattered wings. The green box shook. Buddy, Sunny, Reginald, and Sugar cowered. Suddenly Buddy understood Mad's voice: Each part of each teddy grafted onto her body contributed a mournful tone.

"WAS IT fair THAT I WAS THE one To TRAVEL FAR AND long ENOUGH TO LOCATE THE SUIT? Look AT ME. SEE THE evidence OF all THE teddies WHO CAME BEFORE YOU. I warned each **OF** THEM THEY **DID** not want **To FIND** THE SUIT. BUT teddies **ARE** stupid. THEIR HEADS **ARE FULL** OF fluff. THEY **GAVE ME** THEIR parts **To** FIND HIM. Willingly, THEY **GAVE.**"

Mad's white-on-black grin pulled wider.

"**AND MAD** wants more."

Buddy trembled. "Did any of the teddies reach the Suit?"

"WHO KNOWS? **Teddies, I CARE** NOT." Mad's limbs writhed up her long body. "ALL **THAT** matters **IS I CAN** feel THEM. THEY ARE part **OF ME** NOW."

The teddies shook so hard they shed plush.

"**SO,** teddies . . . DO **YOU** still WISH **To KNOW** Where **To FIND** THE SUIT? IT **WILL** cost **you A** part. One SINGLE part EACH—IS **THAT** so **MUCH** TO ask?"

Soft paws pulled Buddy close. It was Sunny. She'd gathered all four teddies.

"Let's decide," she whispered. "But fast."

"What's there to decide?" Buddy hissed. "We can find children on our own."

"I agree," Reginald said. "There's no way the teddies who gave Mad their parts made it to the Suit. How can you survive out there missing a paw, or a leg, or your eyes?"

"That's why Pookie making it back to Garden E was such a miracle," Buddy added.

The blue and gray teddies turned to their yellow friend. Sunny was staring at a tank top glued to the sticky floor.

"Then what was the use of any of this?" Sunny asked softly. "Of Pookie and Horace dying? Of seeing what we saw in the Store?

This place is the last clue Pookie gave us. If Mad tells us where to find the Suit—it's one more clue, teddies. One more chance."

In a wee voice, Sugar said, "She can have me."

The slithering of Mad's legs was the only sound.

Buddy stared at the pink teddy. They all did.

Sugar—the kindest, sweetest, most optimistic—was the Furrington of them all.

"Mad can have *all* of me," Sugar clarified. "So none of you have to lose any itsy-bits. She can have my itty-bitty paws, and my tiny-winy legs, and my fluffy-snuffy tummy, and my happy-wappy head."

Sugar pushed her tinfoil tiara off her crooked taped eyes.

"My head isn't so good anyway," she said with a shrug.

Buddy felt lifted into the sky, by awe, by inspiration.

How could one little teddy be so brave?

"No," Buddy said.

"Sugar, we can't," Reginald said.

Again, Buddy and Reginald turned to Sunny. Still she stared down at her yellow feet, her soft face wrinkled in thought. Buddy didn't like it.

"It . . . would be a solution," Sunny whispered.

Buddy and Reginald gasped.

Sunny's paw shot upward: *Shut up.* Slowly, Sunny raised her face.

Buddy knew that look. And, oh, was he glad to see it.

It was the look of Teddy Duty.

"What did the last Proto story teach us?" Sunny asked. "You

never betray your friends. You never sell them to someone with no love in their heart."

Sunny put her paw around Sugar, the snug the pink teddy was always waiting for. Buddy couldn't help it: He did the same. Soon gray plush joined them. It was a snug so tight Sugar disappeared into their bellies. Their dirtiness, their wetness, their smelliness didn't matter. Buddy could have held that hug—that snug—forever, until his fur rotted away and his stuffing softened to dust.

"You're not giving up one little stitch on your little pink body," Sunny said. "Now let's get out of—"

The hug was ripped apart. Buddy was hurled against the wall, and glimpsed spiraling yellow fur and tumbling gray. Mad's long arms had flung the teddies apart and had Sugar in their eely grip.

"You forget I have many ears. How perfect a solution offered by this pink teddy. She might be the most gallant teddy I ever saw. A pity, really." Mad's arms curled tight around Sugar's neck, drawing her close. "I think it's time I added a second head. So Mad can converse with herself. Better than constant interruptions from silly teddies."

38

Stitches being ripped from plush.

Echoed inside the box, the awful sound outdid the storm.

Like a raccoon the teddies had once startled in an alley, Mad backed herself into a corner, impossibly tall on her quartet of serpent legs. Her left tentacle squeezed Sugar's body to soda-can size. Mad's right tentacle was clasped around a nail file, probably chucked into the donation box long ago. She dragged the point of it down Sugar's side. White stuffing oozed out.

Sugar gasped.

"Don't look, Sugar," she advised herself.

The pink teddy ripped the packing tape off her face. Her plastic eyes came off with it. The tape, with the eyes still adhered, clung to her paw as Mad raised her higher for another jab.

Buddy and Reginald were shocked to standstills. But the most incredible sight was yet to come: Sunny launching full speed off the heel of an upside-down loafer. The yellow teddy timed it with feline precision, bunching her soft body into a ball before bursting outward.

Sunny hit smack into Mad's chest. The yellow teddy lodged her paws and feet on the teddy ears stitched everywhere. Mad screeched—and the nail file dropped into dirty clothes.

"GET off ME. teddy!"

Sunny scaled Mad's torso. Mad lashed her free arm. It cracked across Sunny's back, knocking one of her paws away. But Sunny held on, found new grips, and clambered up Mad's left side, right below Sugar. Sunny leapt and snatched the dangling piece of tape with Sugar's eyes stuck to it.

Mad roared and twisted. One of Sugar's eyes shook free, lost forever. Sunny grabbed the remaining eye, pinching it between paws.

Buddy had no idea what Sunny was up to until the last second. After Sugar had torn her eyes off in the culvert, Reginald had shown Buddy and Sunny the sharp plastic stems on the back of the eyes.

With all her teddy might, Sunny drove the eye stem deep into Mad's side.

Mad shrieked. The blare vibrated the whole box as well as Buddy's head. It buzzed like a bee swarm, and from inside it, Buddy heard a ghost of the Voice.

Protecting others is hard. It can mean putting yourself at risk.

The Voice, whoever it was, gave good advice.

Buddy dashed, hard and fast, at Mad's legs. Two of them socked Buddy, but he pinballed around until he planted himself into Mad's belly. The plastic teddy noses attached there were unexpected. Buddy felt a teddy's instinct to give them little kisses.

In place of kisses, he twisted one of the noses like a dial. It ripped right off. Stuffing, as white as any teddy's, poofed from the hole.

"What ARE YOU DOING? Stop it!"

Sunny plunged her paw into the slash she'd torn with Sugar's eye. Her yellow paw sank deep inside Mad's guts. An instant later, Sunny pulled her paw out. She had hold of what looked like a thread, but thicker—a thread made of threads. It was what the Mother would call a "seam."

With both paws, Sunny gripped the seam and jumped from Mad's side. With a hoarse noise, the seam tore open the whole side of Mad's body.

Sunny landed atop Buddy, a jumble of yellow and blue parts. Pink parts too—Mad had dropped Sugar. Finally, gray parts, as Reginald protectively hurled himself over his friends.

Mad wailed. Stuffing blizzarded down, all over the teddies. The long, tall teddy fell so hard that items of clothing—a handkerchief, a weight-lifting glove, a baby's christening set—shot upward like clouds of dust. The four teddies clung to one another as the whole green box groaned.

Sugar, eyeless and blind, hid under a woman's slip. The other teddies did the opposite. They streamed over Mad like black ants had once streamed over Horace. Mad's nine eyes shone with green-orange fright.

"Please! I'LL GIVE YOU BACK YOUR FRIEND!"

But they already had Sugar, didn't they? Sunny twisted Mad's left arm where it was sewed to her torso. Weakened from the weight of all those teddy paws, it ripped right off. The plush wing connected to the arm tore down the center, shedding the teddy name tags.

"I'LL tell you WHERE THE SUIT is! GIVE ME A chance!"

Reginald yanked long coils of stuffing from the hole where Buddy had removed a nose. The large teddy's body began to deflate—thinner, thinner, thinner.

"Genesis Way! YOU'LL FIND THE SUIT ON a road called Genesis Way! I'LL tell YOU HOW TO GET THERE! Just listen!"

Buddy had his paws on Mad's right arm. He was going to snap it off, just like Sunny had the left. Didn't Mad deserve it? She'd done terrible things in this terrible place. There was no disputing that.

But Mad's voice now . . . Buddy heard in it the same heartache that had made him and his friends leave Garden E. Perhaps Mad's own failure to find a child had torn apart her heart long before Buddy, Sunny, and Reginald tore apart her body. Buddy stepped away, swatting at falling plush.

"Sunny, Reginald. Stop. Leave her be."

They either didn't, couldn't, or wouldn't hear him. They kept going. Stuffing bloated in the air like dandelion fluff. Scraps of dyed plush covered the floor like a coat of fall leaves. Teddy eyes, noses, ears, tails, paws, and legs piled high and low, a repeat of the Store dumpster's massacre. Buddy waved his paws while Mad's screams grew weaker.

"Genesis Way . . . GENESIS WAY . . . GENESIS . . ."

"She's going to tell us where the Suit is!" Buddy cried. "Stop! Stop!"

But it was too late.

Mad's whimpers went silent.

None of her ghastly limbs moved.

Only now did Reginald look at Buddy. A second later, Reginald gazed down at his chubby belly. It was coated in Mad's stuffing. When he spoke, he sounded dazed.

"I heard you . . . tell us to stop. I just . . . kept going."

Sunny looked equally as stunned. Her yellow fur was spotted with colorful scraps of ripped plush. When she spoke, she sounded lost.

"I don't know . . . what came over me. Buddy? Did we do something bad?"

Buddy looked at his friends. He shook his head. He didn't know. Maybe even little teddies, if hit hard enough, strike back.

If so, it didn't make Buddy happy. Not one bit.

In the silence came a rustling noise. Sugar, still eyeless, wriggled from the donated clothing. Buddy heaved aside a purple jumpsuit, clambered over to Sugar, and stroked her blind face. Sugar didn't ask which teddy was touching her. She wrapped her paws tight around Buddy's legs.

"Can we leave now?" she asked. "I don't want to be here anymore."

IN THE BAG

39

Rain came down like chain-sawed trees. It exploded against the parking lot pavement, which had cleared of cars and loiterers. A few vehicles remained in the drive-thru lane. Red brake lights smeared across wet pavement, as rain whacked roofs and gonged hoods.

Buddy figured no one would notice four teddies slogging along the edge of the lot. They were blue, gray, pink, and yellow, in that order, but their colors had stopped being pretty. Rain had darkened them. Mud coated their stubby legs and rotund bellies. They skirted puddles for a while, then gave up and waded right through them.

It was impossible to avoid getting dirty in this world.

Buddy led the way but no longer felt in the lead. Genesis Way could be anywhere. He had no idea which way to go. He simply kept moving, away from the road, through the rear of the parking lot, and into the trees by the dumpster. The green box faded from view. The Yellow Plastic Hills became obscured by dripping branches.

They entered what looked like a forest, the site of storybook tales, the home of beasts worse than anything in the Haze. It was still night, and they were utterly lost. Yet Buddy said nothing. He felt tired, guilty, forlorn, angry. Any beast they found would be a welcome distraction.

But it was no forest, only a glade. Quickly the teddies came upon a gnarled, broken fence. Its chain links wobbled with rain-drops. Buddy squeezed through a hole. He half hoped the others wouldn't fit. Then it wouldn't be his fault when he led them astray. They got through fine. From there, the ground angled downward so steeply Buddy took pawfuls of weeds so he didn't tumble.

Rain slapped every leaf on every tree, a deafening noise. So Buddy didn't hear the highway until he saw it. He stopped at the tree line. Before him was a shallow ditch, a gravel shoulder, and a gargantuan six-lane road lit by tall orange streetlights. It was sim-ilar to the first highway they'd seen, but even bigger, even louder. There was no culvert shortcut Buddy could see.

Vehicles whooshed in both directions. Headlights exposed cones of rain moiling like wasps. The hiss of rubber tires over wet pavement was the world's longest strip of tape being ripped away.

Buddy searched for the highway's name. But it only had a number.

This sure wasn't Genesis Way.

Buddy felt the soaked plush of the teddies behind them. Left

or right: They were waiting for him to decide. Didn't they know better by now? Couldn't they do anything by themselves?

He stepped out into the rain. He didn't worry about being seen, not in a downpour like this, not at night, not by cars going this fast. He turned right and began walking along the wet gravel. He saw green road signs, yellow warning signs. So many, waning into the black rain.

They walked. Enough time passed for morning to rise, the color of hot steel. The rain slackened to a mist that draped over Buddy like spiderwebs. He kept brushing it from his face. His stuffing was soaked, making him twice as heavy, making every step a chore. Traffic had thickened and pelted him with grit.

"What are we numbskulls doing?" a teddy muttered.

Buddy hadn't looked back since Mad's donation box. But he was tired, uncomfortable, and cross. He whipped around so fast rain jetted from his fur like darts.

The others looked like dirty rags molded into the rough shapes of teddies. They were plastered with wet leaves and grayed by tire splatter. Their fur was imbedded with gravel.

Reginald was Reginald. He stared listlessly at the swampy gravel. His dour catchphrase was swallowed by road noise: "We're not going to make it."

Sugar was in a wretched state. The tape on her face was wet and curling, and the single eye they'd managed to replace gazed off into the sky. Her left side, split open by Mad, was tied shut by shoelaces Reginald had found in the donation box. Having no fingers, teddies were bad at tying knots, and the laces were loosening.

Sunny, however, was glaring.

"Is there something you want to say?" Buddy demanded.

"We don't know where we're going," Sunny growled.

"Of course we don't," Buddy snapped.

"We need a plan. Don't you have a plan?"

Buddy took a step toward Sunny.

"No, I don't. Because you tore apart Mad before she could tell us where Genesis Way was."

"I don't feel bad about defending Sugar."

"Defending Sugar? Or using Sugar as an excuse to be violent?"

Reginald cradled Sugar. "Don't talk about this in front of her."

"Don't worry," Sugar said, her eye pointed upward. "I can't tell who's talking."

"Who says Genesis Way even exists!" Sunny cried. "You're taking the word of a monster with teddy parts sewed all over her!"

"She was a Furrington too! She could have helped us!"

Sunny bumped aside Sugar and Reginald, bounding toward Buddy.

"You were hardly the voice of reason back there! You attacked Mad the same as we all did!"

"That's all you want, isn't it?" Buddy snorted. "You want to drag us down to your level. You want us to be so *tough*. It's like Reginald said back at the Store. Pretty soon we won't even be teddies anymore!"

209

"Don't drag me into this!" Reginald grumped. "You're both acting like . . . like people!"

Now Sunny glared at the gray teddy. "I've had enough from you too. With all your *wisdom* and *knowledge*. If you know so much, why can't you stop us from messing up?"

"Because you never listen," Reginald said. "You're impulsive, you're mean, and you're dangerous. It's un-teddy-like."

Sunny shoved Reginald.

Buddy watched in shock as Reginald landed in the soupy gravel. He tried to get up, but his right paw got tangled in a plastic bag and his left leg stumbled over a shred of tire rubber. The gray teddy had always kept himself tidy and undamaged—and now look at him, splashing in mud, struggling to stand.

Swift as a passing car, Buddy's shock turned into rage. He tackled Sunny. They fell onto a sodden paper plate, rolled over a broken phone, bashed into a crushed soda can. Their limbs were fabric and stuffing, hardly capable of harm, but their fury was real, and Buddy was aflame with it.

Reginald tried to pull them apart. Sunny kicked Reginald. Reginald kicked back but missed and hit Buddy. Buddy hit Reginald, who hit Sunny. Fighting felt as rotten as that old, dead rat festering in a culvert, but also, in Buddy's darkest places, it felt good too.

A lucky punch sent Buddy rolling halfway into the ditch. He stopped himself, shook his plastic eyes free of rain, and scrambled back up, dying to hit again. But he'd lost his place a little and crested the ditch at a different spot.

That's how he saw Sugar wander onto the highway.

Her single eye dangled from the peeling tape. A truck streaked by, so close that Sugar's wet fur fluttered. She held down her tiara with both paws, and so had no balance when the truck's wind spun her into the path of a gigantic RV. The motor home was white enough to be an angel, here to take a teddy soul.

"*Sugar!*" Buddy screamed.

He started to run, but he was too far away.

The RV didn't honk its horn. It didn't swerve. The pink blotch on the road was just one more scrap of roadside litter.

40

Reginald pulled Sugar back to the gravel.

Buddy might be bad at judging time, but he knew Reginald had saved Sugar with a second to spare. The RV shot by with such force, Reginald and Sugar were blown off the side of the road, all the way into the weeds next to Buddy.

Buddy stared at the gray and pink teddies in disbelief until he turned that disbelief upon himself. Sugar had been rescued, but no thanks to Buddy. What if she'd lost her final eye? He crawled closer and rolled Sugar onto her side.

Reginald slapped his paw away.

"Stay away from her," Reginald said.

The gray teddy blundered to his feet and helped up Sugar. Buddy was relieved to see the tape on Sugar's face still clung to her eye. Reginald shoved the eye back into place. It wouldn't hold for long but would do for now.

"Is she . . . ?" Buddy began.

"What do you care?" Reginald asked. "Why don't you and Sunny keep fighting? It's all you're good for anymore."

The gray teddy put his paws around Sugar and started walking. Buddy followed, but slowly and at a distance. He recognized the queasiness inside him. He'd felt it when he'd woken up in the trashlands. It was the feeling of not being wanted.

After stalking past Sunny, Reginald paused and gave the teddy brawlers a look. Buddy hoped for Reginald's expression to show forgiveness. All it showed was disappointment.

"I can't trust either of you with Sugar's safety," Reginald said. "So the two of us are going off by ourselves. We'll find a playground. A schoolyard. Something. Maybe we'll get lucky and some children will decide we're not too dirty."

"Reginald, wait," Buddy said.

Reginald tightened his grip on the pink teddy. "Come on, Sugar."

Sugar waved at Buddy and Sunny. "Too-da-loo, teddies! Ooo, does this mean we all get to be pen pals?"

As Sugar began dictating new pen-pal letters, Reginald marched them off in the same direction they'd all been heading. Right away, the gray teddy faded into the morning mist. But Sugar's pink plush resisted like the sun at dusk, determined to light the world just a little while longer.

Buddy decided his Real Silk Heart was pink too. It beat inside his chest until Sugar vanished.

Sunny took a long time picking rubbish from her fur. Buddy took a long time squeezing dirty water from his plush.

"Well." Sunny was barely audible over the highway.

"Right," Buddy replied.

Sunny peered toward the distant spot where Reginald and Sugar had melted into the rain. It seemed easier for her to speak when she wasn't looking at Buddy.

"I think that's the direction to the trashlands." She shrugged shoulders, once yellow but now brown with mud. "That's where I'm going. At least I know the dangers there."

Sunny dared look back for a second. Buddy was glad it was no longer. When their eyes met, it felt like being shot by a pebble flung by a passing truck.

"Well," Sunny said again.

"Right," Buddy said again.

Sunny faced the horizon.

"Good luck," she grunted.

"You too," Buddy grunted back.

Sunny walked off in the same direction of Reginald and Sugar. She vanished the same as they did.

Buddy found an old box of breath mints and sat down to watch traffic.

He was alone. Not just without-a-child alone. Truly alone.

Was being alone all right? He didn't know. For a while, he wondered if a teddy attaching himself to a child was any different than Mad attaching teddy parts to herself. But it was a dreary thought, and he felt dreary enough.

The mist quit. The traffic thinned. The sun pressed through

lumpy, veined clouds. To Buddy's left, the skyscrapers returned, the ghosts of giants. They looked closer than before. They might still have children inside them. But it was an awful long way for a single teddy to travel alone.

So Buddy walked to the right, the way of Sunny, Reginald, and Sugar.

The weather cleared, but vehicles kept peeling rain off the highway. It collected into a heavy, swirling spray. Buddy could see only a few feet ahead. That was all right with him. He'd known in advance about the Yellow Plastic Hills and Mad, and that hadn't done him any good. Let the surprises come.

Behind the spray, blurry shapes began to form.

Buddy figured it was one of the other teddies who'd stopped to nap. But the shapes weren't gray, pink, or yellow. They were orange. *Dozers,* Buddy thought. *They followed us here.*

But the dozers had been a yellowish orange. This orange was neon. Buddy kept walking until he realized the shapes were moving straight toward him—smaller than dozers, but bigger than teddies. Buddy stopped and waited, letting highway gusts push him around.

The shapes were men. Four or five that Buddy could see. They were dressed nothing like the Manager at the Store. These men wore boots, jeans, gloves, protective goggles, and thick shirts. On top they wore orange vests. The vests were striped with reflective white stripes that glimmered in headlights.

One man was chipping dried mud from a sign with a plastic

stick. The mud fell off in brittle brown plates. The words beneath were revealed.

GENESIS WAY →
8 MILES

Buddy's damp sadness cracked into pieces, and fell just like the dried mud. He stared. He couldn't believe his plastic eyes. Eight miles. Was that far? Was eight a big number? There had been eight Originals, which seemed like a lot. But it hadn't taken long for the Mother to sell all eight. Surely Buddy and his friends had traveled a lot farther than eight miles already!

That's right—his friends. Sunny, Reginald, and Sugar. How had Buddy forgotten his Teddy Duty? It had been printed right on the Furrington box.

I'll be there when you need me.

He had to catch up to his friends. Apologize for fighting. Tell them the good news about Genesis Way. Hope was not lost! Not lost at all!

But the men in orange vests were coming. They walked slowly, studying the ground. Each carried a white garbage bag in one hand. The bags sagged with weight, and Buddy could see outlines of the contents. Garbage, of course—the men were picking up junk. It made sense. Of all the dirty places Buddy had seen since the trashlands, this highway was the dirtiest.

In their other hands, the men held long black poles.

One man was closer than the others. He inspected the gravel and grass. When he saw a soda can, he jabbed it with the black pole.

The pole ended in a silver spike. It stabbed the can.

The man lifted up the black pole and shook the can off the spike. It fell into the white garbage bag. After that, he skewered a limp wallet. An empty bottle of cough syrup. A wrapper from a burger joint. Every scrap the man stabbed went into the bag.

Buddy needed to run, hide, find his friends. But there was no time.

He lay down on the gravel.

The spray from the highway settled upon his plastic eyes. Buddy watched from this obscured perspective as the man stopped beside him. The man was big in every way—tall, fat, strong. He stared down through goggles beaded with highway splatter. Unlike the Manager, who'd had a jerky energy, he seemed calm and quiet.

The man looked over his shoulder. The other men were busy with their own garbage gathering. The man stared back down at Buddy, raised his black pole, and jabbed.

An icy shaft of steel pierced Buddy's belly.

Oh no, he thought. *Not before I can apologize. Not before I can lead my friends to Genesis Way.*

He was lifted into the air. Since waking up in Garden E, he'd longed to be lifted, though not by some cold metal spike. However, the man didn't drop Buddy into his bag of trash. Rain droplets still jumbled Buddy's vision, but he thought he saw the man remove a *different* garbage bag from his belt. He shook open the bag and gave his black pole a firm tap.

"*Another* teddy?" the man whispered.

The spike withdrew, and Buddy fell.

41

And fell, and fell, and fell.

"U.S. REG. NO PA-385632," the Voice called. "Are you there?"

"Yes," Buddy said. "I mean, I think so."

"Here we go again," the Voice sighed. "You're a silly teddy, you know that?"

"Am I?" Buddy shrugged into the void. "I don't *feel* silly."

The Voice chuckled. "One day you'll see it, I promise. I know you better than anyone, after all."

"Because you're the Mother?" Buddy asked hopefully.

"You're persistent," the Voice said. "I'll give you that."

"Are you Proto?" Buddy guessed.

"Still asking all the wrong questions, I see."

Buddy had a hunch the Voice was right. "Am I dead?"

"What do you think?"

"The last time I spoke to you, I wasn't dead," Buddy reasoned. "So I guess I'm not?"

"That's using your noggin," the Voice said. "Remember Pookie's missing leg. Or the big tear down Sugar's side. You think a little poke in your tummy's going to end you?"

"I worried the poker might have hit my heart," Buddy said.

The Voice sighed. "Your heart. You're too focused on that, you know."

"How can a teddy be too focused on their heart?" Buddy sputtered. "A heart—why, it's everything! The Mother made the hearts herself!"

"You think the heart is an object," the Voice said.

"Well, sure. It *is* an object. Reginald's story said so."

Even though the Voice was invisible, Buddy sensed it shaking its head.

"Oh, U.S. REG. NO PA-385632. Do you think you're an object too?"

"Naturally I'm an object," Buddy said. "I'm made of things. The Softest Fabric in the World. Polyester Fibers, Plastic Pellets. Only plastic eyes, though."

"Marble eyes, back in Proto's time," the Voice said.

"I wonder why the Mother switched to plastic," Buddy said.

"Do you think you're worth less because your eyes are plastic?"

Buddy gave it a thought. "No," he admitted.

"If you *were* just an object, it *would* make you worth less. See?"

"Gosh darn it," Buddy said. "Who *are* you?"

"Silly U.S. REG. NO PA-385632. Nothing but wrong questions."

Buddy couldn't see his paws in the void but flapped them anyway. "What do you expect? My head is full of stuffing! Can you give me a hint what the right questions are? Haven't I earned that?"

"I suppose you have done pretty well," the Voice laughed. "For a teddy."

"I'm waiting," Buddy said.

"All right. I'll say this, and nothing more. You keep asking who I am. It's a fair question, but you'll never figure it out until you answer another question first. A more obvious, more important question."

Buddy thought. He thought so hard his head stuffing ached.

"I think the question is," Buddy said, "Who am *I*?"

Buddy believed he heard the soft, distant sound of clapping.

"Well done," the Voice said. "You're on your way, U.S. REG. NO PA-385632."

Who am I? What a question! A teddy ought to be whatever their child wanted!

He gave it some thought. He supposed he was a Furrington Teddy, and he supposed his name was Buddy. His name tag insisted it, and the back of the tag listed the name the Voice kept using: U.S. REG. NO PA-385632. What else was he?

He was a friend.

"You miss them, don't you?" the Voice asked.

Buddy nodded. He did. All those things he was made of— the fabric, the stuffing, the pellets—felt twisted up, and it wasn't because of the metal spike.

"We should have stuck together. It's only eight miles to Genesis Way. We could have gone there together." He sighed softly. "I wonder if we can be friends again."

"Silly, silly, silly U.S. REG. NO PA-385632," the Voice chided. "You're about to find out."

42

Buddy awoke. The world went from ink black to cloud white, from tranquility to lurching motion. His blue body bumped this way, then that. He felt the taut, shivering plastic of the garbage bag, but also other, softer things.

"He's awake," said a familiar voice.

Morning light glowed through the bag's thin plastic.

Crammed next to him was Sunny.

"Good morning," she said. "Well, *morning*, anyway."

Sunny had a new hole in her lower left belly. The hole was small and neat, and leaked a tuft of stuffing. Squeezed next to Sunny was Sugar. She had an identical hole in her right paw, poked by the same spike. For once, the pink teddy didn't look happy—she was curled into Reginald, who sat at the other end of the bag. He had no holes at all.

"How do you keep avoiding damage?" Buddy asked.

"I was the first teddy the man found. He used his hands."

Buddy inspected his own puncture hole. He'd lost a bit of

stuffing. In fact, he noticed the bottom of the garbage bag was filled with the teddies' lost stuffing. The top, meanwhile, was twisted shut into a knot. Both sights felt familiar.

"I've seen this place," Sugar whimpered. Her eye, barely taped on, wobbled.

Yes—that was it. The second of Sugar's visions.

I see stuffing inside a twisted plastic nest.

Buddy looked at Sunny. He could tell by her concerned stitches that she'd figured it out too. They were in a whole new kind of trouble. More than ever, they needed to work together, despite their past disagreements.

Buddy carefully stood. The bag bounced, tossing him back on his tail. He decided that was fine. A leader didn't need to stand tall to act tall.

"Sunny. Reginald. Sugar," he said. "First of all, I'm sorry. I'm so sorry."

The other teddies shared glances. None of them looked angry. Sunny smiled tenderly.

"While you were napping, Buddy . . . or whatever you were doing . . . all the rest of us did was pray you were okay." The yellow teddy shrugged. "We're the ones who are sorry."

Buddy might be a small blue teddy at the bottom of a stuffing-filled bag, but he felt the size and strength of a dozer. He wasn't finished. Not even close. He'd get his friends, and himself, out of this bag all the way to Forever Sleep.

"Listen," Buddy said. "I saw a sign for Genesis Way."

Sunny bolted upright, only to get bounced back to her tail. "What? Where?"

"Near where we all got poked."

"Why . . . that's wonderful!"

"It is," Reginald agreed. "What's *not* wonderful is we're being carried away from it."

Buddy pressed his plastic eyes against the plastic bag. He could see arrays of colors on the other side, vivid in the sun, but none clearly enough to make out shapes.

"How long have we been in this bag?" he asked.

"You know teddies and time," Sunny groused. "A minute? An hour?"

"Can we get out of here, please?" Sugar pleaded. "Pretty-kitty-snitty-please?"

The trashlands had been full of torn garbage bags. They couldn't be hard to rip open. Buddy pressed his paws around a fold of plastic. But it was slippery. His paws were slippery too.

The bag bounced harder than ever before, then again, and again. All teddies were tossed together. Their soft parts mashed. Their plastic parts clacked. Buddy felt another puff of stuffing exit his belly. It kept happening: bounce, bounce, bounce.

Buddy realized they were going down. The bounces must be stairs. The air got colder. The sunlight grayed. Bulb light, low and sinister, glowed like torches.

Sunny panicked from under Buddy's back. "Are we back in the Store basement?"

Reginald replied from beneath Sugar's legs. "We're nowhere near there."

Buddy pressed his face to the bag again. He couldn't see anything now, but he heard plenty. People—lots of people. Buddy felt their body heat, smelled their sweat. Some talked back and forth. Some spoke to tinny, metallic voices that mumbled back. A few talked to themselves in a way that didn't sound healthy. One loud voice crackled from an overhead speaker, but to Buddy it sounded like gibberish.

This might be an unwise place to escape the bag.

A low rumble grew in volume.

"Reginald, what is that?" Sunny asked fearfully.

"I have no idea," Reginald said.

The teddies embraced in a damp knot as the rumble grew into a roar louder than any dozer. Through the plastic, Buddy saw a streak of light. The bag rippled, blown by an abrupt wind, and twirled in circles from its twisted stem.

The man held on to the bag with no trouble. He moved, and instantly the teddies were in a different space—smaller, brighter, and so packed with people Buddy felt their hands and hips nudge the bag.

"It's a train," Reginald whispered.

"A train *underground*?" Buddy boggled. "How is that—"

The train, if that's what it was, heaved into motion, thrusting stuffing into the teddies' faces and squashing them into a ball. The speed evened out. They disentangled. But they didn't move too far apart, just in case.

The trip was a long, bizarre one. The train stopped and started more times than Buddy could count. Eventually enough people got off that the man was able to sit down. He placed the bag of teddies between his feet. Buddy stared hard through the plastic and saw loafers, sneakers, sandals, and high heels.

"Shoes," Sugar sighed, for some reason comforted.

The train was scary, and yet its vibration and noise were oddly relaxing, like being rocked in a cradle. Buddy was nearly napping when the man picked up the bag and hurried off the train. There was a sensation of rising along with hazy glimpses of a silvery surface Reginald speculated was an "escalator." The sun burst back to life, as bright and surprising as being hit with a pail of yellow paint.

That still wasn't the end. Next came walking. After that, a bus, which was like the train, but brighter and slower. After that, more walking, down a street squawking and clanging with bells and alarms. The man's pace grew slower as he went. Buddy wondered if grown-ups also feared what the future might hold.

A door opened and closed. Dark again. The man climbed stairs that creaked, and creaked, and creaked. At last he stopped. He inhaled. He exhaled.

"You can do this," the man whispered.

Buddy didn't think the man said it for the teddies, but he decided to pretend. Buddy *could* do it. They all could do it. They just had to stay calm. The best way to do that, as Sugar might say, was snugs. Buddy reached out and got the snugging started. The blue teddy held the gray teddy, who held the pink teddy, who held the yellow teddy.

Keys jangled, a sound the teddies knew from the Manager. They also knew the metallic crunch of a key turning inside a lock.

So far, the man had only whispered. Now he shouted. His words made Buddy think of his own first words: *Is anyone there?*

"Hello, fam? It's me."

43

Behind the white plastic, Buddy saw the man's boots. He'd set the garbage bag on the floor again. Unlike the train or bus, this floor didn't shake.

Buddy did his best to look through the bag. The light was softer. They were indoors. It was quieter. It was warm. Smells abounded, though none were as pungent as those of the trashlands, or as sickly as those of the green box. Buddy smelled things his teddy mind was built to identify. Soap. Potted plants. Burnt toast. Hot tea.

An idea came to Buddy, smaller than the fresh hole in his belly.

The most wonderful, implausible, absurd idea.

The man had taken them *home*.

Buddy shoved his plastic eyes harder against the bag. He saw spindly things. Legs, but not of people. Chair legs, table legs, sofa legs. He turned, the plastic rippling smooth over his plush. He saw a shelf with CDs on it. He saw a shelf with books in it. Until now, he'd only seen such things broken and tattered in the trash.

Most incredible was a bright, flickering box. Buddy didn't need Reginald to tell him what it was. It was a TV. And who had TVs? Families did. Buddy felt dizzy. He reached out for support. Sugar happily hugged his wandering paw. Sugar, that astounding teddy! Her second vision had predicted this path, bringing them to the most glorious destination of all.

A creak came from above. It was dark up there, but Buddy felt pretty sure the big man had sat down on a chair. The bag of teddies was stashed beneath it.

"Don't everyone say hello at once," the man grumbled.

"Hi, Daddy!"

Buddy gasped. Sunny gasped. Reginald gasped. Sugar squeaked. There was no mistaking it.

Oh, Mother—they were in a home with a *child*.

"Hey, darling," the man said.

Catlike steps pattered across carpet. A shadow smaller than any Buddy had seen on the train or bus frolicked by like a pony. The child's smell washed over Buddy like the spray from the highway. Milk, candy, grass, the sweetest sprinkle of sweat. It was a girl, Buddy identified. A girl! And her name must be "Darling." What a wonderful name!

Darling launched herself against Daddy.

"Mama," she cried. "Daddy's home!"

"Darling," Daddy said. "Why aren't you at school?"

"Good question."

This new voice had to be Mama's. Buddy and the others spun

in wild circles, trying to locate her. Unlike Daddy's soft chuckle and Darling's high-pitched peeps, Mama's voice was stern.

"Third time this quarter," Mama said. "And does that girl look sick to you?"

"Aw, she always looks good to me," Daddy said. "Takes after her daddy."

Buddy could hear the love. He could smell it; he could taste it.

"She *plays* sick." Mama snorted. "Got that from Daddy too."

"I've been working hard all morning," Daddy sighed. "Don't lay into me just yet."

"Daddy, you hungry?"

Darling's voice was spinning crystals and crayon rainbows! Buddy had never heard a grown-up conversation before, and he couldn't really follow it. But who cared? He understood the little girl perfectly.

"Working?" Mama asked. "When a judge makes you pick up junk on the side of the road, they call that 'community service.'"

"Yeah, yeah," Daddy sighed.

"You should have lunch with us, Daddy."

Darling's voice was sugar-cookie sprinkles and satiny hair ribbons! But her parents' disagreements were scratching off some of her sparkle. The girl sounded a little scared—and a lot sad. Buddy realized that made *him* feel scared and sad too. Is this what it was like to have a child?

Buddy thought of the magical pop of static electricity that helped the Mother bring Proto to life. That's how Buddy felt:

alive, electric. *This* is why he'd been born. *This* was the moment he'd been waiting for. This child needed the comfort of a teddy. And no teddy could supply comfort better than a Furrington.

Under the chair, he thought. *Little girl, we're down here!*

"Nothing I do is good enough for you," Daddy muttered.

"And it won't be until you're fully employed and clean for good," Mama said. "Until then, you don't get to act like some hero to my daughter."

"*Our* daughter," Daddy corrected. "And I've been clean for two months."

Buddy was struck with dread. Daddy wasn't clean at all! His boots and pant legs were slathered in dried mud. His orange vest was splashed with highway filth. His shirt was muggy with stinky sweat. Daddy was lying, and Buddy fretted. What if Mama made Daddy leave? What if Daddy took the teddy bag with him?

"Mama," Darling said meekly. "Can't Daddy stay for lunch?"

"No!" Mama snapped. "Daddy *cannot* stay for lunch."

Fast and frigid silence flooded the home, and the bag too. Buddy was appalled. A home was supposed to be loud with laughter and the click-clack of toys. This was the same kind of bickering that had split up the teddies beside the highway.

Daddy spoke softly. "Let my darling spend time with her daddy, huh? Just a few minutes?"

The floor shook as Mama stomped away. Buddy heard a door slam.

Daddy sighed.

"Go on," he said. "Sit next to Daddy."

Buddy saw Darling's feet climb onto a chair.

"Are we having lunch?" she asked.

Daddy sighed. "Afraid not. I made Mama mad again. I'm just going to borrow this jar of peanut butter, all right? If Mama notices it gone, tell her I'll replace it."

"Okay, Daddy."

The chair over Buddy's head creaked as Daddy adjusted.

"Now, listen," the man said. "I have a surprise. I know Mama lost Roo. I know how much you loved Roo—"

"Is it a stuffie?" Darling squeaked.

Stuffie—Buddy felt dizzy, jubilant. It wasn't a word he knew, yet he knew it meant *him*.

"Shh," Daddy said. "Mama can't afford a new stuffie right now, but that's not her fault. It's mine. I screwed up."

"Daddy!" Darling yelped. "Gimme!"

"The last thing Mama wants is Daddy giving you gifts. So you have to keep them secret, all right?"

"Okay!"

"Do you promise? I'm serious, now."

"I promise, I promise!"

The garbage bag crinkled. For a manic second, Buddy panicked. Too fast! He wasn't ready! But when the bag was lifted into the air, and Buddy flopped onto a bed of his own teddy stuffing, he had to stifle a laugh. Of course he was ready. He was a teddy. In moments, he and his friends would be removed from this bag, and their tough, troublesome lives would fade into Forever Sleep.

All four teddies whispered at once.

Buddy: "Here we go—"

Sunny: "Right now, right now—"

Reginald: "I can't believe it's—"

Sugar: "Finally, finally, finally—"

They all shut up. There was no time. Without a word or thought, they pressed into each other, the tightest, most loving snug of their short, incredible teddy lives. Only three words were spoken. There was no telling which teddy said it. Maybe all of them did.

"I love you."

The bag was set gently upon the table. Buddy had an urge to jump for the twisted top, but he knew the time for moving around was finished. *Lie still, teddy*, he told himself. Forget Mama's anger. Forget the Voice saying Buddy needed to figure out who he was. Forget the Suit. Forget Genesis Way. Buddy's Real Silk Heart was throbbing, and that's all he needed.

"I don't know if a box of them fell off a truck or what," Daddy said.

"Open it!" Darling begged.

"You're going to have to clean them with soap and water, but only when Mama's not around."

"I will, I will!"

Plastic rustled. The bag shivered. Buddy went limp. Ready for deliverance. Oh, Mother, ready at last.

The sky opened up.

Heavenly light blazed. Whiter than white. A hole burned through reality. It was the opposite of the dark void, the place the Voice insisted was Buddy's home. The Voice was wrong. Right here, right now, *this* was Buddy's home.

A dark shape eclipsed the luminous glare. It was a pigtailed head lowering itself in front of a ceiling lamp. That's all. The most normal thing in the world. Yet the most glorious thing Buddy had ever seen.

Darling's face was soft and round. Her eyes were brown and sparkling. Freckles cavorted down both sides of her nose. Her mouth opened to show two missing teeth. Her smile was so big the corners of her lips touched long, springy pigtails.

"It's teddies," she gasped.

Darling reached out toward them.

Her little hands, spotted like flower petals from watercolor paints, opened wide. Her fingers, striped by mishandled crayons, wiggled in delight. She reached into the bag.

All four of the teddies were going to get their Forever Sleep.

So Buddy decided it was all right to stop being a selfless leader. Just this once, he wanted to go first. He prayed to Darling, to Daddy, to Proto, to the Mother, to the whole world, the same thing he used to pray in the Store: *Pick me. Pick me. Pick me.*

And it happened.

Darling's hands settled upon Buddy. Her soft fingertips sank into his softer belly. As she lifted him from the bag, he felt the dried mud on his plush crack to pieces, followed by what felt like the cracking of his Real Silk Heart. *It's happening*, he thought as he was sailed through the air.

The girl brought him closer. Her smile, the gleam of her teeth, the sparkle in her eyes, together they were brighter than the sun. Buddy was blinded as much as Sugar had ever been. He felt the warmth of Darling's sticky cheeks inches away. He smelled the grape candy stuck somewhere in her teeth. He felt the first teasing tickle of her curls. Her hands folded hard into his back.

Darling, a real human child, hugged Buddy.

He felt his plush body flatten with the force of this child's quick, absolute love. His plastic eyes pressed against her sugary skin until he saw only blackness. Was *this* the Voice's black void? Was *this* the home the Voice had described? Buddy let every worry squeeze out of his body, like dirty water from a washcloth.

He waited for his life to slip away, a feather stolen by a breeze.

The blackness kept going.

The hug continued.

Buddy was happy, the happiest he'd ever been, until the hug

ended, and he could see again. Darling was setting him down so she could pick up the next teddy.

Buddy's rear end landed on the table. He tipped over onto his face. He was staring down at a stained tablecloth. He was in shock. He could barely think. Had the teddies done something wrong? Had everything they'd known been a lie?

The Forever Sleep, that release from strife and pain they'd been promised . . .

. . . it had not come.

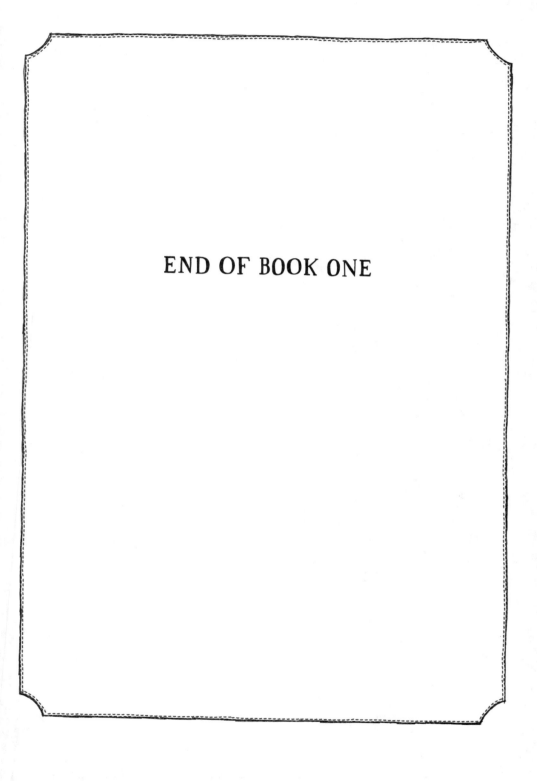

END OF BOOK ONE

ACKNOWLEDGMENTS

Thanks to Richard Abate, Tara Altebrando, Michael Burroughs, Rovina Cai, Daniel Handler, Dana Kaye, Ann Kelley, Katie Klimowicz, Amanda Kraus, Kelsey Marrujo, Mark Podesta, and Christian Trimmer. Finally, to Richard Adams, whose *Watership Down* I read in a large-print edition (the only copy my library had) when I was a kid. That book changed a lot of things for me, and as will be obvious to any fan of it, the Teddies books reflect my sincerest gratitude.

972
MAR
C/1

Marx, David F.
Mexico

$14.95
BC#34880000074091

DATE DUE	BORROWER'S NAME
11 13 30	Bria W
207	Sebastians

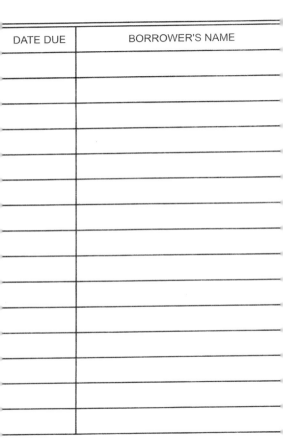

DATE DUE	BORROWER'S NAME